Amongst Giants Revealed

JEFFREY ADAM

Fulton Books, Inc.
Meadville, PA

First originally published by Fulton Books 2018

ISBN 978-1-63338-766-9 (Paperback)
ISBN 978-1-63338-767-6 (Digital)

Printed in the United States of America

Contents

Part 1

Amongst Giants Revealed

You Are

June 26, 2017

You're the song bird before dawn, a sound of hope
You're the dew on the peddle, my reason to cope

You're rain on a summer's night, the fertile ground I stand
You're the sun that gives me light, the warm summer sand

You radiate love, give without asking, and hold nothing back
You're the cool autumn breeze; you fill the space I lack

You're the sparkles on the water, diamonds shinning bright
Church bells ringing clear, you give this blind man sight

You're the fresh grass below my feet, while I run and play
The moonlight in the sky, turning blue skies from gray

You're the oxygen I breathe, the answer to a prayer above
In the desert you're the water, you're the epitome of love

You're the downward slope when my knees are weak
The Song of Songs I'll forever sing, the everything I seek

The calm snow falling on a winter's night, a Snow Angel
The fireplace that warms me, you're Heavens every angle

A foundation, a cornerstone, the rock upon which I stand
A shooting star shinning ever bright, I'm your greatest fan

You're a book I can't put down, a mountains highest peak
Your words are soft and gentle, kind and most unique

You're the reason for this poem, flowing pen and paper
Energy giving new life to all, I will never give in or waiver

When you leave a part of me will die, always in my heart
From the moment our eyes met, right there from the start

You're the blanket on a winter's night, the Truth I pursue
A clear summer's day at sea, with the most marvelous view

The anchor for my ship, the anchor for my heart and soul
The lighthouse that guides me home, the bountiful bowl

You're the canopy that shades the sun, cooling my being
You're the reason I fight, standing ground, never fleeing

You're strong in mind, body, and soul, reaching for the stars
I pray at night because of you, you're in my heart not far

You're the honeycomb, the secret spice that life supplies
The sounds of crickets cheeping at dusk, the glow of fireflies

Silks, fine linens, perfumes of elegance could not compare
You finish ahead of the pack, into your eyes I forever stare

Nothing in this life but you withstand the test of time
So if you ever feel down, remember this poem, this rhyme

Anxiousness

August 10, 2017

Anxiousness fills my inner being; the day light slips to night fall
Shorten breaths I take, fear fills my thoughts, listening for the call

The day reminds me of promises you've made, hope in every drop
Coincidences' most will say, but I know better, I will never stop

I prick my finger on a thorn, spill a drink, or hear that certain song
That whisper in the wind, cool breeze,
knowing you're there all along

Why? I ask, the shouting keeps me awake, will this ever end, I dread
Waiting upon the world to sleep, when we'll you come like you said?

Nothing seems to fill in the gaps, only
the prophesy and the promise
Pictures and reminders just won't do, I'm
Peter, I'm Paul; I'm Thomas

I need someone whom believes, all around
me have no Faith, nor will
Gods are created by the media, moving at the speed of light, not still

Everywhere I look and go; sacredness has been left behind I grieve
Looking to the skies above, I pray for
someone, something to believe

I stomach tight, my heart sinks, I'm tired;
my tears I cannot hold back

Is there someone, anyone out there to hear,
to listen; to the things I lack?

I weave this web of lies, my bed in shambles;
I toss and turn, never sleep
Knowing you're always there listening, this
prayer tonight I forever keep

Hidden close to my heart, love will win
ousting the darkest of nights
These heavy burdens I ever hold within, burst to flames, for I fight

I'm idle in my response to your call,
wasting time, waiting for the end
Truth is, is that I've never been in control
with a plan, or had a true friend

Seems years have speed by, one less in the passenger seat, I'm alone
I'm tested day in and day out, fingers crossed, as I wait by the phone

A call that never seems to come, all I have
to blame is myself, my effort
Never taking a chance, I'm frozen, had
true love once, should've kept it

A coin lost, a treasure without a location,
a map without a key or lock
Prevailing winds never seem to whisk me
there, laughed at and mocked

I'm talking to myself once again, answers known, advice never taken
Swept by the undertow, I may be pushed
to the edge, but I'm not forsaken

The seas are rough, the waves at the highest
point, pinnacle, and peaks

You're somewhere out there waiting upon
me too; it is me that you seek?

Do we know each other, are we friends,
acquaintances, or are we strangers?
Is there fate involved, are we destined to
fall in love; medicine or a cure?

What I know is there's an absence, my feet
fail through the desert sands hot
Sun beating without cool water to drink, I
thirst, there's a story line, a plot

The maze full of dead ends, twist and turns,
I fall upon bended knee, I pray
There's nothing shameful bowing down to
God above, under his sky I lay

Monsters scroll through the pages I look
upon, her curves catch my eye
Fraudulent master plans from the deceiver,
fallen angels to earth from sky

Dancing, moving in sync across my mind,
images dead upon our stares
Consequences we do not render, nor are
we mindful, do we even care?

This night will not be devoured by such rot;
the drug will not enter my veins
For help is on the way I trust, a partner to
keep me safe, warm, and sane

Relax, keep calm, keep cool, know the dawn
will breathe new life and hope

I repent with each waking moment; my
    weakness and failures, I must cope

I've been sober for many a day and night,
    his grace is sufficient and enough
I take these wise words upon my lips and
    heart, though the seas are rough

My diary screaming upon the pages, my
    words violent, holding nothing back
Virtue is from our creator above, the grays'
    are excuses; it's white and black

In between is where we find comfort, we
    tell ourselves we have a right
We give to the rich and rob from the poor,
    we're blind; we've lost our sight

An hour left until we turn another page, a
    new day begins from an ending
Patiently, as if I had a choice, these prayers
    upon the pages I'm now sending

A gift is never null and void, when sent with
    care you will receive an answer
One must be careful what they wish, for it
    may result in death or a cancer

A wolf wrapped in sheep's clothing, a lie, a
    farce, bringing you to the edge
Dared to step upon the waters black, promised
    the world, step off the ledge

I'm wearing out my stay, I must leave soon,
I'm in the way; I'm a burden
I ache within with every heartbeat I take; I
look outside through the curtain

Time waits not for anyone; the young are
naive and ignorant to its existence
I don't claim to know it all myself, but I do
know I mustn't have resistance

Where is the sacredness? Where is the
modesty? Where is the prudent one?
Have we been abandoned tonight into the
cold abyss, are there any, some?

Ticking seconds and minutes lead to the
hour, on the other side I await
I neglect my responsibilities, my aspirations,
chancing my certain fate

I argue and try to justify, pleading to the
world I'm not what they think I am
They call me stupid and witless; I start to
think I might be, sinking sand

Can I inspire? Can I use my gifts and talents?
Does anyone see anything in me?
Can I point anyone in the right direction?
Can I stay in the moment, not flee?

To be content with yourself is a gift; to be
at peace with yourself is divine
Learning to love yourself is the hardest
thing I've done; this is certain sign

Forgiveness is right around the corner, she
lies filled with poison and death
It takes her veins as we speak, needle to the
spoon, like the pipe to the meth

Words are far and few between, she has
nothing left else to hold onto here
We haven't spoken in a year or so, the only
thing we have in common is fear

Does she sleep, or does she stay awake,
pondering all that's been stripped away?
Soberness versus drunken binges, both asking
our self, should we go or stay?

What if the roles were reversed? Could I
pry myself out of certain waste?
Would she make an effort to reach out to
me? Tears upon the pillow I'd taste

I once was trapped like her, nights screaming
without a sound, hollow soul
Wishing to be led into nothingness for
eternities end, feeling out of control

The truth is I can't change what is now the
present, time will separate, move on
The future starts now, the new day has
change, righting out what was wrong

The fight has just begun, my friend; the ink
has run out for now upon this night
Though her battle comes now to a close,
your opportunity has brought sight

So in closing words, her final breath inhales
and exhales lifeless her body lays
Remember one day you'll meet again on
the other side, at the end of days

Justice Finds No Reason

August 11, 2017

Justice finds neither reason nor rhyme through a maze thick forest
Days lasting eternity, sickened hopeless lives guarded by fences

Imaginary hills surrounded territory, rock thick, steel cold to touch
Fortresses built to last a thousand years, bombs burn and blaze

Trails of filth fill the skies, pollution chem-trails seep into the night
Prison camps file up the zombies, brought together as one unit

Fields of poppy, the drug takes the vein,
guarded by the American soldier
No questions asked, blood money traded for a soul by the deceiver

Soldiers told to do without question, labels placed upon our society
Black, white, gay, wrong or right, there is
no wrong, and you have no right

Filth on the screen, the papers, the
magazines, Hollywood is cancerous
Do this, this is the way, be yourself, don't follow the beaten path

Cheap pornography, uncultured, classless
society, witless, opinionated
Child molesters watching our children play,
teaching them in classrooms

They are our teachers, education a dime a
dozen, degrees out of a cereal box
Handed out like candy, in college debt for
years to come run by a broken system

Trillions of dollars wasted, dollars backed
by unpaid debt, paper notes
Images of the enemy taking center stage,
staged burning of buildings by us

Creating illusions, deceiving our own people,
feeding them what they want to hear
The land of the free, home of the prisoner,
land owning slaves, no possessions

Stock markets artificially pumped up by
steroids, bankers laughing on their way
Leaving the poor right where they're at,
middle class is a big joke, my friend

Music beats synthetic, nothing original, hope
I do not place here on earth or man
Talk is cheap and so is war, presidents,
kings, dictators write the rules

Pretending as if we go a make a difference,
leaving a trail of mythology left behind
Remember God doesn't sleep; we walk in
drunkenness day and by night

Raping woman, children, leaving our own
on doors steps left to die and suffer
Terrorist walk the streets in civilian clothes
and so do our own soldiers

Who is right, who is wrong, truth is we
are all just as sick and twisted
Christian, Muslim, one god, or multiple,
we lack structure and direction

Gold, possessions, houses, wins over losses;
this is how we judge each other
Everything seems to be just a game, laugh in the face of our brothers

Computer engineers, nurses, doctors, lawyers on every street corner
These are what we call jobs, a dime a dozen,
years upon years of college debt

Politicians in the game for four years, suck
up lobbyist's laundered money
Laws made upon laws, amendments lost, exceptions to the rules

Killing the innocents, the new genocide,
babies the size of dimes disregarded
Placing wedding bands around the enemy's
finger, our lives demoralized

Mixing iron and clay together, false creation
not by our Lord and Savior
God above on high in a rage watching
down upon our lack of judgment

Elite families plotting the fall of man, we breed
each other out, melting pot society
Gathering up us pigs together in pens, the
power and their control their bliss

One world order, secret societies, watching
over us as we kill each other off
We run into the fire without any hesitation, like moths to the flame

They know our patterns, they watch our
movements, guilty until proven innocent
The stars no longer shine in the night sky,
pollution, deforesting takes over

Space program, nuclear program, technology
taking over our working environment
Computers in our hands, instant gratification,
answers all in one moment in time

Arrogance, ignorance, belittling, pleasure
in our hate and upon our lips
Stabbings, shootings, hate crimes and words
cutting, suicide grips society

Staged deaths, cover-ups, masses persuaded
by the mass media combined effort
Dictator after dictator promising a better
tomorrow, death chamber awaits

Natural disasters, rising seas, threats of war
permeate from all around the world
All keyed upon the land of milk and honey,
wipe them off the map, they say

Words twisted, manipulated, forged in
Hell's fire, watchful eye in the sky
Plans have been figured out, use this as you
will, my prison is my own mind

Their Pain My Happiness

August 31, 2017

The air seems different tonight, moon
shining brightly amongst the stars
Planets all aligned, synchronized by the hand
of God, red in the sky is Mars

Questions flicker across my mind and the
universe, why so much turmoil?
Hurricanes, torrential rains gather historically,
lives ruined, crops are spoiled

Here on the flipside, calm night brings forth
peace, tranquility, so hopeful
Tomorrow is the next step in the process, new
beginning; I pray it is not foiled

Why does he give me so many second
chances? I always seem to fall short
Though tired in my own right I trot on, knowing
that I may at one point get hurt

The page flips and I'm tired, worn; I'm weary
in this fight always comparing
Patience is my enemy; never credit myself
for accomplishments, not caring

A new era begins, new opportunities, though
so much pain is all around me
My dad in shambles over my sisters' disease,
hells gnashing teeth, I now see

Unveiled are my eyes, the scales fall to the
ground, the cool night wind, shadow
Trees bristle in the dark late summer night,
waiting for the change to follow

The night sounds give way to bliss, the moon
glows orange and yellow, so high
Ranging from east to west chasing the sun,
following the ruler through the sky

For once I'm serene, new hope fills my
thoughts, childlike excitement glowing
Praying it's not too late in this life, I ask the
simple question, where am I going?

I've lost my sense of belonging; work seems
to be slipping away from interest
What I once desired with ever increasing
passion is now gone, all in fairness

The love has faded; everyone has left and
soon will be leaving, should I stay?
I ask myself this simple question daily, is it
time to move on, I'm in disarray

I'm in such conflict between the other side
and the fight in this place we call life
There's got to be much more to this than these
pages, I give everything, my strife

The races of my life go on, one after another,
I ask myself when should I stop?
I pray not to lie to myself anymore, there's so
much I've achieved, I mustn't rob

Steal the truths of my gifts to the world, though
poor compared to the rich man
I am rich with love and truth, character the
bar I set for myself, distances I've ran

I will go to the ends of the earth for my love;
I've seen the response in her eyes
I've seen the passion she feels for me within,
I've felt her heart beat and her cries

The days fade slowly like a painter including
every last detail onto the canvas
His nights spent by the light of the flame,
looking for contrast, certain conquest

Looking up into the heavens the rain pours
down with the playing of the song
He's in the moment you see the shooting
star you've been waiting for so long

I fail to be a good witness; I hold back my
experiences, so coy, so reserved
Fear of judgment and abandonment fill my
being, soon I will get what I deserve

Tonight my fellow mankind sleeps not as I
join them, losing all possessions
The storm ravages their lives, ripping their
worlds to shreds, life's hard lessons

The question isn't anymore, do we deserve
this? Or, is he getting his revenge?
We've made our decisions now we must
make the next step, my voice I lend

For his furry will be unleashed, though I
will live like there's no tomorrow
I will not live in fear; I will live for today with
both happiness and with sorrow

The paths twist and turn, meticulously
bending every which way and pattern
A new day holds firm, new paths, new ideas
gather like wheat to the cistern

I don't want to miss a thing, so I wait for the
moments to happen without rest
I beat myself with the reed, crown myself
with thorns, God can surely attest

Forgiveness is my foe, my archenemy, I
have trouble letting go of the past
For I'm the least amongst this pathetic
kingdom here, and surely heavens last

He will find me, I will be ready when he does,
I will grow in strength in season
These coming days I will grow in awareness
and wisdom, finding sure reason

I can feel it in the night air, in the speech
amongst the trees, the earth calling
Speaking to me in the many tongues, whispering,
he will catch me when falling

I am not afraid anymore, all has been taken
from me, I have been humiliated
Walked through the streets naked and mocked,
my soul has been disintegrated

Now in this final verse she speaks so clearly,
it's not about me it's about him
She prays for me in this moment, then, now,
and tomorrow, for all fellow kin

Early Autumn Morning

September 4, 2017

Justice unfounded by ignorance, man justifying his every error
Reformed thinking, in the blink of an eye, labor pains we endeavor

The time has approached, the moon losing ground chasing the sun
Glowing wild ambers lighting up the celestial night, slowly it fades

Gray skies, like rushing waters, wind furiously moves across the lake
Bleeding into a calm starry night, quiet and still, the creator makes

Peace in a word a hologram, fading memories of yesteryear as child
Playing on the playground, unity once a
priority of my life, now wild

Wildfires growing ablaze, once surrounded
by friends in every corner
Now alone with his thoughts, his nights
pouring his soul of his former

Former being, once so rooted in rocky ground, soil blistering so hot
Fertile ground is what he seeks, all these
years in his head he has fought

Demons demanding his soul, ripping his
hardened nights of sleep and rest
For what shall one hold on to in the bowels
of hell, what shall one caress?

Hunger fills his belly; knowledge evades
his mind, twisting his thoughts
Overload of information, too much to
grasp within his fingers he sought

In our minds we make ourselves gods,
everyone neither right nor wrong
The times of the final season is upon us,
the years are shortened yet long

Seasons come and go; rain beats down on
the roof on a cold dark night
While time ceases to exist on my time
table, early autumn moon bright

Am I coming or going, comfort I avoid;
never content with the moment
The ticking clock, pangolin swings with
the flickering stars high above

Colorless wind brings forth smells of campfire choking on the ashes
Coarse black smoke fills the tear dropped
air, controlling all the masses

I avoid resting my head in fear of being
left behind, I lay cold and naked
Shivering in the dead cold of the early
autumn morning, nothings sacred

For we've sinned, I lay here ashamed of
my actions, our decadence fades
In my passion I find furry and rage, the truths
of my God, my Savior I evade

Patience is all but gone; anger and vengeance
embrace each and all of man
I feel the absence in every cold heart, my
finally plea, firm ground to stand

The pull of my senseless actions, deepest,
darkest desires are unfulfilled
For illusions for my guilty pleasures of lusts,
dancing shadow, picture stilled

Heavy burdensome heart, lonely days and
nights, sea of ocean, lips parched
Fresh water to drink is unobtainable, distant
shores out of sight and vision

The calendar frozen, pages fail to be turned
in fear and ignorance, God's word
His lips utter phrases of hope and peace, yet
he turns a blind eye, it's absurd

Man's thoughts can be so burdensome,
sweeping dirt underneath the carpet
Ignoring certain facts and truths of our
hatred, wrongs, even how it started

My head is heavy, my eyes wide awake, these memories I try to avail
Our children no longer have respect nor
prudence, for this is why we nailed

Our Lord upon that tree, the Cross, we
neglected to open our eyes to see
The children once again misguided fortune,
Judas runs to the desert to flee

Dark forces now gather together, surrounding
my existence, body burning
I feel the flame upon my bruised and battered
body, my soul now churning

Like the prophets of old they mock me, they
laugh at my hypocrisy, failures
I hate the sins of man, my own and theirs
alike, though humanity I care for

I will succeed, I will carry on, move forward;
we will go back home soon
For the yoke of my Savior was not all in
vain, he has made us all a room

I am the least; the dust of my bones will
gather up and be made whole, anew
For suffering also is my call, though sometime
near I will be part of the few

Blessings

September 6, 2017

Exhaustion fills my core, flesh to flesh, bone to bone
Anxiety runs rampant, thoughts of temptation, I'm alone

He steps through the door, thoughts not making sense
Boiled blood spilled over, it's hard to see through the lens

Blinders put upon my eyes, seeing only half the picture
Conspiracies clutter my days and nights, part of the fixture

Another year approaches an end, the same, different views
A house built upon a hill, safe from the storms of new

They wait in the shadow, counting all my mishaps, misgivings
Virtue avoids my being, what does it to mean to know I'm living?

The storms are unleashed upon earth, I will not give in
Throwing in the towel is not an option, even amongst my sin

I seek an outlet, to relieve me from these sinking feelings
My ship is taking on water, obscuring me from all I'm seeing

I know he heard me cry all these nights, I still ignore the call
Blaming everything on everyone else, just waiting for a fall

The morning night sounds, crying out louder than before
Selfishly I await the peace of night, for what is soon in store

I see the starry night at hand, the blaze of stars across the sky
The smells of campfire amongst the night while angels sigh

The stir of the early morning rises, winds blowing strong
Tonight we sail on stormy seas, praying it won't last long

The call of the Lord is mighty, I recognize him in the eye
Where winds are the calmest in comparison, tears I now cry

The evil one is lurks in the shadows, my Savior gives me strength
It will not end this night, my friend, I now will go to great lengths

My story has just begun; the riddles are upon my pen and lips
The hunters and gathers meet for feast, no longer clinching fists

I count my blessings tonight, while I wait upon the rising sun
These years upon the lake will soon fade; further will I run

My sword has been sharpened; lighter, stronger is the blade
Forged in heavens care, going soon to where all sin fades

I hear the call, it's louder, more persistent than it was before
It fills my whole being and self, I know now what this life is for

To give him praise, exalt him overall, fight the fight for all
To live, to die, to breathe for him, for he has broken every fall

My words are my enemy time and time again, head is pounding
This moment I realize his strength, he's for me, glorious sounding

My right hand forces the keystroke; my left holds back a thought
Fear is what keeps me awake at night, all that's safe I have sought

The past is now gone; I must take a stand if only for the truth
I'm growing old within this skin, losing hope from my youth

This small town holds a tight grip upon me, back to the beginning
To where it all began, I wish to rest from all those whom are biding

Betting for my failure, boastful of my shortcomings, falling down
They snicker all my days pointing fingers, shaking sacred ground

Moving forward is all I have left, humbleness is what I seek
For the misfits and failures will rise, the earth inherited by the meek

I must trust this moment forward; I've lost all I had yet nothing
For I travel light without a possession, having God is my something

To lose what I never had would be nothing less than a blessing
For the curse is in the wallet, having wealth in heaven is resting

Small-Town Girl

September 10, 2017

Sun methodically starts to fade; bright lights start to spin forth
The crowds gather in cluster, waves like ships arriving at the port

The evening starts with chatter, friends gather from all around
Drowning their worries and fears away, taking in all the sounds

She looks at him in passion, yet doesn't know his name or story
Something sparks her mind to conversation, both courage and glory

The intoxication takes her mind, laughter presses on, doesn't know
She thinks she feels with her heart, the moon above shines like snow

The sky on parade not for all, observing he looks all around to see
If she only knew his past and present would she want to know me?

Realization and truth matter, one with
God, nature, and all to behold
Knowing who you are the key, knowing what you want is control

I'm locked in my room with these demons; she's free as the birds
With confidence she dances in the night, her words are just words

She grasps on each lyric and beat, holding her head close to his chest
Wanting something that seems out of reach, searching for her rest

She'll wake up this morning, come to her senses and move forward
For a chance with the dark prince would be crucial, he is a coward

I spend my days in denial, eyes all around me watch in judgment
Being just a face in a crowd of many an entirely different substance

When the soberness of the morn hits, will
she respond with eagerness
I already too clearly know the answer; I sit here reacting in weariness

The afternoon wears on; the communication
rises, intriguing thoughts
How to make the next move on the chest board, information sought

Seeking to feel out each other, wondering what could be and or how
Leading one to believe could be fatal,
living in the moment, the now

She's been alone all these years wondering, who will raise my boy?
Am I alone to do this job and task? Should I stay, or should I avoid?

This couch has been my solitude, my
alliance; these nights my enemy
For my thoughts and actions avail my
duties, distraction is my remedy

What shall either one of us make of this, both awake tonight restless
He's been waiting much too long for a way out, part of the checklist

The truths and the secrets becoming
disconnected, like land to the sea
Boundaries of nations out of alignment
with constellation; us, or we?

The two phrases similar but detached,
divided, separated into groups
Categories forming alliances, friend and foe, bringing one for a loop

Can two so different beings coexist? Is
there any way to bring together?
Should even any miniscule chance be
attempted to wait out the weather?

Worlds collide tonight, this most obscure
connection, bond, or truce
What are the odds of lightening striking
twice, or go on, what is the use?

A small-country girl, seeking for a diamond
in the rough, few miles away
Does fate play a role; is love at first sight
a myth, leave tonight or stay?

Time will truly tell; I have all the time in
the world, it's in his hands free
For I am on his watch around the clock,
safe in his arms in where I be

My hope is in his knowledge, his foresight,
knowing the future, beyond
It's happened already I know, using good
judgment, I've waited so long

Tonight we are separate, tomorrow leads
to new opportunity, new hope
Here in this moment is the new beginning,
a new way for us both to cope

For she looks at him with passion, he
looks at her with contemplation
Looking for a reason to move on forward,
to avoid just mere temptation

To Adam

July 5, 2017

4 in the morning, demons crowd my mind I'm fully exhausted
Memories of our conversation twist and turn, my mind is haunted

Sadness rips apart my soul, the words so close upon my lips
My mind falters and stumbles, my heart so heavy I can attest

Peering into the windows of your soul, mind, and inner self
Questions and answers aren't so certain, losing all earthly wealth

Can government answer our problems? Can assistance be the key?
Is there something more than this, where our brethren can flee?

A home just beyond our reach, where we run and will not fail
A place where we don't need vice, grounds do not shake nor we bail

Thoughts collect in my mind, lyrics spew forth from your being
You make all laugh with joy, reflection within seems all I'm seeing

Will hope prevail over the darkness, something beyond the stars?
Where minds aren't cluttered with haze, we don't have to reach far

Heaven is real to me, though sadly this place we call Hell burns too
I wish to one day meet you on the other side safely with a view

A view we can both be proud of our children while we'll gather
As one at the table, but as I sit here now no one could be sadder

My friend, it's not enough to forgive, it's not enough to be kind
The reality is that our enemies are just like us with similar minds

They want what's best for their children, to be safe and secure
Though some want the world to burn, but for now we must endure

You say that my soul is light, and that I'm genuinely most kind
But hear me say in this moment only in Heaven I will only truly find

Myself saved through trail and fire, forged within flames so pure
For I have claimed Him as my King, my one and only Savior

Without my testimony I would cease to exist without any cause
For we're all sent with certain purpose, though we have many flaws

The call for lesser government, to be ruled by the people within
The corruption of politicians and their greed controlled by their Sin

We the people ruled not just by one, but by the whole as a unit
Under one God we trust, the weak to the strong, we're all students

History repeats itself, generations suffer without certain awareness
Nations come and go; the blame is on each and every one of us

Back to the beginning, a new revival, hope is where we shall start
Self-reliance is a farce without a king, an illusion without a heart

The night has bled to day; the music of the morning fills my ears
Questions fill this inner shell of doubt, releasing all my inner fears

Terror and horrid painful imagery, filled my dreams in the night hour
Though now the day approaches with light, to evil I will not cower

In these closing thoughts, I would lay my life down for a friend
So if I had any say at all, both our broken hearts are on the mend

It's Hard to Say Goodbye

July 29, 2017

Seeing you walk away saddens and breaks my heart, I cry
Thinking of all the times we've shared both watching the sky

Looking watching the snow fall, wondering, talking out of turn
Not minding the interruption of the other, smiling no concern

You always keep me in wonder, my breath and lips quiver
I tremble with anticipation; you're elegant and always deliver

I'll miss your eyes of fire, brown, warm, your soul exposed
Those moments you vent, fire in your soul, thorn to the rose

You give me reason to write, sleepless nights I lie awake
Thinking of a way to impress you, my heart is true, not fake

Words written down as imagery, a song to one I care for dearly
I would stop the world for you tonight, one can see this clearly

You're the center of the room, the light in the darkest of places
Especially within my heart, shine the brightest amongst all faces

I light up when I see your car, when I see you walk with grace
I become like a child with awe, the most dreadful day you erase

You'll always be in my heart, a vivid picture within my mind
Within a frame made with care, you're a perfect catch and find

He truly is the luckiest man; I'm envious of the treasure he holds
You're soft glowing ambers on a winter's eve with a heart of gold

The memories we have can't be taken away, they're mine to keep
Going for coffee, for pizza, to church, and running, with joy I leap

Country music playing, you're a perfect picture captured by time
You're the cool summer breeze, the shade on a hot day, my rhyme

I could never forget your face; I smile ear to ear in your presence
Knowing I won't be able to see you for a while is my prison sentence

You tell a story like no other, fine detail, I could listen to you forever
Passionate beyond measure, full strength and courage, you endeavor

I struggle to find words, for nothing is
enough to describe your being
You're loyal, intelligent, intellectual, wise, giving all of us meaning

You move me like no other has ever had, now I sit here and ponder
You're water in the middle of the desert;
you're the awe and the wonder

I'm a fool when it comes to you, weak with
nonsensical manner and way
You're the stars on moonless night, turning
the darkest dawn into day

Do not fear now, for I pray for you at all times without ever ceasing
Wherever you are I'm there, for you are
a gift from God and a reason

Though you may have wanted to walk
away at times, you stayed instead
I'll always be in your shadow, to the land
of milk and honey I am led

I wish to embrace you, feeling your warm touch, colors of your soul
Days of driving to nowhere, nights
watching the stars, to never let go

You'll be gone soon and my heart will break, but please don't forget
I would die and suffer a thousand times
over, for this I will never regret

Spirits Lost

August 3, 2017

Peace, love, tranquility; our God has no use for compromise
False prophets all around preach emptiness upon all kind of lies

He will louver one in with a smile and a hand to hold on to
Both standing near the edge will both push you, and bound you

He will tickle our ears, heighten our senses with glorious signs
We will bow down to his image, turning our backs is our crime

Relativity, his first love, it's your interpretation, how you perceive
Unity is his farce, miracles miraculous in sight, the web he weaves

Star readers, tarot cards, and cheats feasting upon emotion we seek
We mustn't pray to spirits lost, for we will truly crumble, we're weak

I stand watch on this damp night, waiting for the true God's return
He will come like a thief in the light,
lighting the world on fire to burn

The deceiver's motto is coexistence for all;
there are no rights or wrongs
The truth is right before our eyes: he's the
host of host, and all the psalms

These trials before us at hand burn us clean, we must stay awake
For his time grows short, his furry is in
the forefront, our lives at stake

We are to understand the times, hate the crime, the time is at hand
Brother, sister, and child we must leave
behind, their homes in the sand

Don't look back, you will be sift out like wheat, blood to the harvest
We must bow to our true God, we must
get up now, travel the farthest

The day will come where the song bird will sing no more, silenced
The moon will fail to shine, sun darkened,
stars fall, then the violence

The head shot will be fatal, but he will
return with awe, mere illusion
The world will be a disarray and shock,
there will be much confusion

Artificial peace will cover the land and waters, blinding our eyes
Forgetting the God of Abraham and Isaac,
falling angels from the skies

The deceiver is here, are we willing to
fight, die, and suffer for a cause?
I've seen him in the city, standing in a Holy Place, giving me pause

He's the magic trick, your next fix, the release, all earthly pleasure
A meal ticket, the easy way out; with him
you won't have to endeavor

We mustn't give up our bonds, our loyalty, and trust put in above
For a false sense of temporary security, for a false sense of love

I want pure light, the smell of fire, fireflies
in the night sky on display
Breeze in the forest on a summer night, a drop of rain and a ray

A ray of hope, a ray of light, our God coming down as he promised
For the Holy Spirit to consume me once
again like I'm making progress

Set me ablaze Lord, steadfast in your love, not afraid of consequence
To be able to stand up before hatred, not faltering in his arrogance

Give me faith; give me strength, patience, fire and gifts to endure
Show me your truths, your certain coming
wrath, what this life is for

You both know my thoughts; my words will be used against me
For one of you spews out death, filled with cowardliness and envy

So the dawn is at hand, the light approaches
slowly as a new day begins
You cannot hold down what is for certain, for the Lord always wins

I've seen his face; I've smelled his whiskey breath, rot in his eyes
He is the host of all cancer, black hole sun; he's the lord of the flies

Red Moon

August 7, 2017

I've been on watch for years; I've been on guard, looking to the skies
Soon he will return catching me and the world on fire, the rest will
fly

The words on my lips fail me evermore; terror fills filth upon their
ears
I waste my time frozen in fear; sadly I have been dormant all these
years

Peace comes about me on this quite night, the fading moon red with
glow
Unusual feeling within my being, the still calm waters stirred by the
row

The signs are all around the night sky, creation, nature cries in unison
Though I want to run and flee, let go, I will not let myself be
worrisome

Anxiety mustn't win us over, for the war and our debt has been paid
These demons that clutter all around me now, through waste I have
wade

The future at our disposal, the wait, the awe is gone, so sad to be
Instantaneous gratification is now our passion, distractions we do
not see

I embrace what is true; I've seen it in the eyes of the poor and meek
We must take the time to listen, for angels of all forms daily we now
see

We're all here now, the time has come; the battle plans are now set
The days and times have been foretold, promises we mustn't forget

My words fail expectation, my heart, my strength wear thin to the bone
Though trials I have faced, the intensity amplifies, I sit here all alone

I've been place amongst murders, liars, stabbing with deceit of all kind
I try to let my God shine through me, they laugh and mock, the stars align

The negative charge within the air pushes me to what I feel is most safe
Avoiding conflict, feeling ashamed, I'm worn, weary, hiding in my cave

I've seen heaven, I've seen hell, I looked upon and into both of their eye
Though you do not know what I've encountered, know that I tell no lie

Comfortable within our lifeless bodies, daily ventures lead to emptiness
Asking ourselves what this life is for? Repeating the cycle of insaneness

We fall into the scams, smoking death, drinking poison, consuming hate
Sex and pleasure is our god, minds rot with illusion on screen, it's too late

Time has stopped, the choices have been made, which side do you stand?
There's no turning back now, we've come together numerous as the sands

The critics will soon speak, their venom, their slander; the script to the tee
No place to rest my head here, my friend, look to the sky, bow to your knee

Coming in the clouds, sword in his mouth, slaying the deceiver and his kin
Blood knee-deep in war, the soldiers have no power, only shame and sin

Cunning is her words, softly spoken, eyes leading young and old to believe
Destroying all that is sacred, losing all self-control, webs of lies are weaved

The whore sleeps well tonight, waiting to dig in her teeth into the next victim
On seven hills he awaits, faulty promises of hope, fornication is a symptom

He's in bed with her, she whispers softly in his ear the next move in place
Allies have all but disappeared; the only thing left now is to reveal his face

Red moon takes over the night sky; soon it will be full to the naked eye
Then the motion will be put forth, moon blackens out sun, woman now cries

A prophet I am not, but I foresee this certain truth be told, hold it close
Rules have been thrown out of play; we're stabbed by the thorn of the rose

His Creation

August 11, 2017

Letters written, years pass by at the speed of light, world on axis
Tilting in unison with the morning star, space time continuum

Distances between planets of rock, some
frozen inhabitable conditions
All created for a purpose, created for our existence, our eternity

Vastness of space, infinity, immeasurable calculations unimaginable
Miracles all molded and shaped, forged
in the fire, massive explosions

Black holes, quasars, stars die creating life, elements for his creation
The hand of God, building blocks, shaping using natural formulas

Pondering our meaning, our desires, our needs and wants, our goals
Why were we created? What is our purpose?
Common questions of man

Physical bodies with invisible soul, guided
by a presence beyond our belief
Our minds cannot fathom or ever equal his
ways, his hand guides all creation

Man manipulates and forms unnatural
structures, hybrids, false gods molded
Our intellect forgetting our creator, the
miracles of the past just mere fiction

Piecing together our own conclusions,
ignorance of false allies, man mislead
Illusion, dimensions, unseen to our two
dimensional vision, deductive reasoning

Concluding by hypothesis, things we cannot
understand, tricking our minds
Possessions, net worth, the goal of the human
ego, power the only thing left

Obtaining knowledge from the center tree in
the garden, promised by the serpent
A single cell, they say is our ancestor, hawks,
trees, ants, humans all from one

I lie we have been told, my friend, use your
intellect, know this cannot be true
Is it too hard to believe we were made for
him in six days, seventh to rest

The holy bible giving us an outline and
guide, truth and prophesy foretold
Evil demons cast from heaven, distracting,
misleading our certain purpose

The chosen people now is all mankind, the
races must come together as one
We cannot do it alone, or live on our own
island, withdraw and isolate ourselves

All roads lead to Rome, changing our natural
resources chemistry for power
As the world sleeps, the plan is set; the evil one has no organization

His time is limited, we all are here; God holds
the galaxies in the palm of his hand
The universe is his own, his power is unequaled;
the power of Satan is limited

Though his time is short, the furry and anger
is now unleashed upon the earth
We aren't going anywhere, my friend, the goal is to leave us behind

For us to choke on the ashes of hell's fire
poured out upon our blue planet
Formed by spheres of rocks colliding together millions of years ago

Explosions beyond comprehension, beyond
any reason, rational only to him
The moon formed, giving us tides, putting
the earth on axis, changing seasons

The snow, the rain, the smells of the forest,
life giving waters, and manna
Bread from heaven, given in the desert to the
chosen, rock spewing forth water

Iron cores, only for our own good, we
cannot fathom or explain why?
The speed of light, slowing down space and
time, stars dying out giving light

The blackness and reversal of space, both in-between growing apart
One day will come back together, time we
cannot count with calculation

Time is in his hands, past, present, and future is what sets him apart
Knowing the evil one's moves ahead of time,
letting him have some power

Though many will be damned, the few
whom have been faithful will rise
Time has stopped and is running short; we
mustn't give into hate without hope

Intuition

August 12, 2017

Night wind howls, eerie stillness followed by clouds filled city lights
Human versus machine, computer chip
internet worshippers, false hope

Passing by each other, empty smiles, eyes
glancing, disregarding thoughts
Conversations lost for eternity, battles forged
in still time, we're distraught

Hollowness of hearts, forgetting our
sympathetic intuition and emotions
Reacting on what we've been told to do
instead, programmed, controlled

Blood is in the water, our fathers of past cry
out from the grave with warning
Letters left in fictional format leaving out
certain fact, we're all conforming

White noise fills my days, evenings, early
morning, sounds scream immensely
I cannot avoid the ravage seas arise, fingertips
bare to the bone; my only escape

Humming of the television screen, sickening
my stomach, aching feeling within
I feel his presence surround my freedom, the
ignorant laugh, dismissing their sin

Disregarding their own intent, making
exceptions to rules forgotten over time
Books written to tickle their ears, pornographic
scenes paint the pages in between

Twisted double meaning of words and phrases
fit to fill in the missing pieces
Giving rise to doubt and fear among ants
marching, follow or destroy the leader

Where does one go to hide? Mountains, caves,
and valleys, from God no escape
The blinds and shades have been drawn, secrets
have been revealed, this our fate

Moths consuming possession, drawn to their
execution administered by the fires
Escape is not an option, choices are pure
nonsensical, his jealousy I admire

Confidence betrayed by weakness, we give
in to the mousetrap games played
Falling, shooting stars fall down from the
heavens tonight unseen and voiceless

Autumn approaches, change is in the air, for
those with freewill we do not fear
For rumors of war are stirring up among
mankind, we're distracted and veered

An imaginary god, hidden from the eyes of
our youth, unspoken by our society
Parents live in illusion give their children
candy instead, don't rattle the cage

In the field, in the work place there will be
two, one snatched away the other left
In wonder and shock, terror engulfs their
being; we're alone now, left in the pit

To the king and queens of earth he will be
introduced, steady hand and bow
Leaders tremble in horror of his wisdom
given from the creator, we will know

Stubbornness will consume them; plagues
run rampant throughout the earth
Egyptian pharaohs like yesteryear will
dismiss the charges, man will suffer

For now the writer watches over the flock in
secret, nights spent alert, on guard
Summer slips through the clinching tight
fingers, patiently watching from afar

He looks upon their faces, they age with every
moment; time is quickly halting
Nothing last forever only love, this is pass on
as the gift given to him from birth

Songs fill the empty corridors, new and old
alike, what is first will be last, surely
Psalms fill the church on Sunday morning,
the angle voice sings from the pulpit

He ponders whether or not to indulge, get
involved; take a chance one last time
His eyes out of focus, his heart beats fast,
voice unheard, seeking for a sign

Choir gathers together as one, shame is his
enemy, days of past creep up slow
The deceiver knows she's somewhere out there,
he's ready to devour from below

The goal is to dismantle the church, generations
forgotten and lost by design
Foolishly he is swayed to give pieces of the
puzzle, in a dazed and confused state

Honey to the bee, horse to the carriage, man
to his wife, Jesus to the church
One cannot separate fate, the pull and changing
of the tides move in sync in time

Predictability, deductive reasoning, misleading
the witness, our own children
I watch in disbelief, words are manipulated,
made to fill an agenda, faulty plan

Give and give, rewarding nonproduction,
idleness with malcontent, malicious
Behavior unacceptable, they put out their
hands for charity, hearts are vicious

Wondering if he is the one foretold? Time will
tell, counting the moments given
God knows the seasons, the fruit is ripe, ready
to be picked, repent; we're forgiven

The morning comes without hesitation, upon
us a new day, a new hope, new life
Cancelling out but not disregarding the
significance of our sign and my own strife

The grain has been divided, the oppositions
brought together upon the battlefield
The battle soon approaches, but for now he
has been sent for all to divide and heal

The hour has come, the time has brought
forth the final hour, and the final day
My son, my boy, you will see your true father
this I promise without further delay

The Assumption

August 15, 2017

She's called out in the dead of night, John racing to her with fear
She panics knowing the time had come,
her memories of him so dear

He's brought before a farce council; accusations, lies fill the room
Denied by his own apostles; Peter thrice, the rest we just assume

They scattered, frightened of what may
come to them, Jesus left alone
His betrayer cold sweat dripping down
with doubt, to the hill he roams

Mother left alone discouraged, stomach aches with unbearable pain
Sickened to her very core she looks to
Heaven asking was this all in vain?

Beaten, battered and bruised, led into
the prison cold, left over night
Hanging from the chains below, awaiting
certain fate, never losing sight

Mother cannot sleep, fervently praying, never ceasing, blessed of all
Looking to Heaven above, asking to give
her son strength, not to fall

Torturous time, slipping what seems like
an eternity, awaiting mock trial
She nursed him from his very infancy,
wiped away his tears, all the while

His body ripped apart by sickened men,
never blaming them for their sin
Holy Mother watches on distraught;
sentenced to death by his own kin

Crucify Him, Crucify Him, they shout,
while tears fill her face and eyes
Thoughts of when he was a young man she
recalls, this moment asking why?

Led upon the streets, laughed at and
mocked, punched, and spat upon
John leads her closer and closer getting one
last look, what had gone wrong?

He looks into his mother's eyes; with all
his might he tells her this phrase
Mother, I make all things new again! Because
of this eternal life, I praise!

Nailed upon the tree, through his hands and
feet, hammering over and again
Left there in agony for hours, she looks
upon the Cross, all because our sin

Anguish consumes her soul, her life torn to
shreds, watching him fade away
After he dies and is laid in her arms she will
suffer immensely too many days

Weeks and months pass by after his
resurrection and rising into heaven
She is left to only remember the years spent
with him, bread raised to leaven

Our Lord looks upon her with passion, love,
raising her up once and for all
For what we call the Assumption is real, my
friend! Never again shall we fall

5 in the Morning

August 20, 2017

5 in the morning, I cannot sleep, sounds of the night alive
The sun rising ever so slow and steady soon will arrive

In sync with the universe, never failing, giving us life whole
I nervously await the new coming day, I'm never in control

I never have been, the creator has everything within grasp
There's nothing he doesn't see, this life wasn't meant to last

My hands and face wrinkle with time, bones are getting old
I've seen too few sun rises because of drunkenness, soul sold

I cherish the moments now, watching sunsets, awe in creation
Snowcapped mountain tops glisten white, satellite station

The moon set in the heavens, perfectly ruling the night sky
Phases never ceasing to rest, perfect circle until he's satisfied

Creation singing songs of worship, all throughout the day
The horizon now lights up slowly, the songbirds now play

The time has come, the night will never again sleep or will I
For our prayers return without void, every tear I have cried

We will no longer thirst or hunger, his bread of life is enough
We are born into a new kingdom, we're diamonds is the rough

The fight is within my mind, body, and soul, constant pull
His promise is great and true; with him I will always be full

Full of grace abundant, saint's intercession, prayers from above
Giving me strength unimaginable, this thing they call true love

The first song of the early day has arrived, he calls out to me
Graciously my heart gives thanks and praise, for now I can see

I walk in faith, each step is guided by heaven's angels most high
For with him by my side always, I will never have to ask why

I will not walk in fear through this unknown valley most deep
For he lives in me now and always, my heart he forever keeps

The second songbird sings, he's closer to my door, open heart
She told me once, live with a heart wide open, never apart

The third songbird sings more beautifully than all the others
I wish to be by her side always, never having an eye for another

The chorus now begins; they call each other the night still sings
Their praises reach heavens heights, as church bells start to ring

Though this moment wasn't meant to last, these eyes sill soon see
For the day soon will arrive like promised, into his arms I flee

Birth Pains

July 13, 2017

A tapestry, picture, a novel set in time abroad
The fire within burns slowly, the leader a fraud

Like the pains of birth, the disorder takes the mind
Blood soaked black with death, no reason or rhyme

Nights silent without sound, sight and senses dimed
Daylight waits eagerly, brother to brother and kin

Lost at sea, waves crashing down, lighthouse in the distance
Calling me upon the shores of rest without any resistance

Uneasy hands and heart, sweating inner doubts and fears
Uncertain call of uncertainty, whispering lies upon my ears

This body dies, this flesh dissolves, and this mind will falter
The strength is from above, no doubts around the corner

Four corners and winds of the earth and seas will prevail
Calling all nations to unit, and never again to ever fail

The moment comes unforced, thoughts are not so random
For the earth speaks out so loud, trumpets all in tandem

Lies are called upon Truth, eerily the images are unveiled
Sitting upon a storm drain, the Devil started to wail

I sat with him at the table; He was sly of hand and of feet
Idolatry, inner wooden gods, demons of the night I meet

Friends are foes, their thoughts are so mindless
Mistakes multiply; we're hypocrites, nothing more or less

The alcohol poisons the brain, numbed is the soul
The drug sets in the vein, hot amber and the coal

Ignorance will lead to death, forgetting all that is important
Our blindness will make us stumble, the disease set rampant

For I have looked into his blackened eyes without Truth
His reign is almost over now, a thousand years of youth

Youth disguised as lies and beauty, using sex is the god
His last wink is here, Truth will prevail, ruling with an iron rod

Ordinary Hearts

September 26, 2015

Faces passing all around, the days blend spinning gray
Another dreary ending, my heart so torn and frayed

Emptiness I'm feeling inside, I look for understanding
For someone to relate to, firm ground in which to lay in

They all seem to be the same, just ordinary hearts
Beating without care, I look to begin and for a new start

Laughing making new memories, pictures still in time
Walking hand and hand, your face so warm and so kind

Jitters fill my inner being, joy consumes my soul
To see you walk into a room, I seem to lose all control

To discover your hopes and dreams, talking till the dawn
When the light brings new day, the bird sings a new song

The glass shoe may not fit in the end, but trying is a must
Never knowing without trial, before we frail turn to dust

I now sit here alone, my thoughts clouded with this fear
We seem to be so afraid, never knowing where life steers

So maybe we can take a chance, before it all passes by
Gazing at the stars together, shooting stars fill the sky

We can wish upon the night, to bring hope for our tomorrow
The hourglass now runs, happiness replacing our sorrows

Maybe you'll say yes, but if you decide to walk away
Know this heart that beats within, will never turn or sway

Goodbye Friend

July 21, 2017

The world falls into deep sleep, he stares into the abyss
The night wind blows warm, all he ever seems to do is resist

Temptations fill the innermost desires, he awaits his move
In his room avoiding rest, innermost thoughts are construed

Hiding the pain in his chest, they're fooled by the smiles
Actors fill the picture screen; they all seem to be in denial

Artists paint the canvas, writers write the screenplay and role
Songwriters write the words they live, death steals their soul

Made to conform to their thoughts, childhood striped away
Needles fall upon the floor, the slayer comes without delay

Change we're told to accustom to, what to wear and when
Drum to a drummers beat; sing the song they want you to sing

They look upon you with cutting eyes, you stand there naked
Judgment placed upon your actions, walk through life, and fake it

Here's a house, here's a car, how 'bout the world and more?
Gold beyond your dreams, all the riches bundled up and stored

He kisses his children good-night, he enters that abandoned room
There seems to be nowhere out, all he had has been consumed

She contemplates her next move, the floor cold with tears
Thoughts hang like lead upon her shoulders, here only a few years

Holidays alone, the alcohol enters her veins, numbing the mind
Shortened days without expectation, looking for anything, a sign

Frustration and lies fill the inner ear, mistaken identity so lost
The station changes but the thoughts remain, counting all costs

Her mom distant doesn't hear her cries, such a shame but true
The evening drew so dark and cold, darkened by night the view

Will they fly one day? Will they perish, or be sent to the fires?
Is there any promise at all, knowledge of the Heavens can acquire?

Old, young, in-between, no person in the world could ever know
A treasure chest tightly sealed, slowly looked upon and bestowed

Questions, contemplation, overlooking what's before our very eyes
The pages stick together wet with ink, all they hear are the lies

One screams with a voice, one screams falling upon deaf ears
The two are intertwined and in sync, the fire is hot and sears

Now I ponder these thoughts and curses, I listen to their cries
Thought silenced by their passing, another star tonight now dies

Falling without grace without end, time and space is now warped
I look upon my own life now, my faults and failures all assort

Money, coins a fraud, treasures fade, dust to dust we will all return
Medal twisted to conform, kings give wills on paper that burns

Born with nothing at all, self-made, she taught herself at best
Forgetting that we're not our creator, creating our own nests

Their names I will not forget, they will never fade into the night
It's why I was created and born, for now, today, and forever I fight

I Wait for Him

July 22, 2017

I wait for him, sleepless nights, dreams vivid in mind
My pen never silenced, lusting eyes the only crime

Restless, worrisome, weary beyond belief or compare
Watchful, sober eyes pressing forward into the night I stare

Cars fill the night's streets, chasing till the light of day
Cheers from the drunken minds, all seem to be in disarray

Thieves hiding in shadow, scornfully mock my every move
Waiting upon my failure, waiting for me to come unglued

Alone on this night I wait patient once again, time stops
Eyes opened wide upon the ceiling, their minds all rot

There is no light upon the sky, the winds move silently
The water still without sound, though my mind shakes violently

White noise fills the hallways, keeping me sane and at bay
Light flickers from the lamps glowing bulb, thoughts are array

Pain fills my body, tears well up upon my eyes and cheek
Though souls go on, my body burns and I am most weak

I listen for the last trumpets sound, looking to the sky in the east
For a sign, an answer to a prayer, for us to be called to the feast

I know I'm saved, but sadly I will be left behind for task
The bowels of Hell shall not prevail, I'm the very least, I'm last

All pride has faded, though hope has regained much strength
For my eggs are all in one basket, He has gone to great length

Preparing me for the storms, testing me upon the flame
Making a mansion to reside, for eternity he will ever reign

Though now I sit and wait, patience is my friend and foe
Silent screams in an empty room, he is the only one that knows

Have I worn out my welcome here? Paranoia fills my mind
What will they think of me? My sanity I look to seek and find

Do they laugh when I not in the room? Pointing fingers in disgust
Saying that I'm just a failure, hanging my head low they cuss

I wait, I sit, I pray for change, for my Savior to return to thee
I look into the darkened night sky for a sign to run and flee

My time has run out, my days shortened to save us all
He soon will call them back home, but here I try not to fall

We're waste upon the fields, sands upon the shores of the sea
Nothing in significance to scale, please open my eyes to see

Artificial light shines, water fails to fall from our cloudy skies
Pollution fills the skyline, hungry children fall to sleep and cry

I wait, I sit, I ponder, wondering when will he come and arrive?
I fail to do my part in turn; that is where the problem lies

Church bells ring on the hour midnight bleeds into early morn
I haven't slept in what feels like a year, I'm tired, spent and worn

I pray my fear will relinquish, joy fills my soul in anticipation
For sadness to disappear, to just exist upon the Lord's creation

But now I sit and wait, for my time to come forth and orate
To proclaim his word to common man, the times have set to date

I rest now, knowing sleep will not come, tonight I stand watch
For it is not my moment now, truth is what we seek and sought

Guidance

July 22, 2017

My guidance is the morning light rising in the East
My way is the Truth and Life in which we all seek

My prayer is of love, the kind no sword can kill
My labor is the fruit he gives; the peace in my soul is still

Early daylight brings forth new life, silence so serene
The songbird cannot hold back songs pure and clean

One's happiness is contagious, one voice lifts the choir
Two voices sing in sync, in unison set the audience on fire

I'm thankful for a second chance, for a sense of freedom
I wait in anticipation to reach the highest peaks, to see them

Angels and Saints eager to greet me, souls forever touched
No powers of hell could hold back, his grace is enough!

The depths of my mind spew forth the lines of his plan
The plans are held upon my sleeve, finally finding dry land

Watered by the skies above, flowing from the eternal fountain
Never running low or dry, for this we can always count on

Forgiveness a gift indeed, a lamb slaughtered for our Sins
Grateful for his outreached heart of gold, and his loving hands

Breaking bread, sustaining life from within our brokenness
For he beckons me to one day return, ridding all my loneliness

I see you in the flowers upon the field, the dew upon the peddle
I see you in a child's eyes, innocence never again being a fable

You're the vast depths of space, exploding suns and stars
Space and time mere illusion, always in control, never far

You're a direct line without delay, you speak on my behalf
You take my words and make them prayer, you spark my laugh

My cries you hear intently, whether joyful, sad, always true
My story and life are in your hands, I'm saved because of you

You're the wish I make upon a star, the answer to a call
The light rising making new day, firm ground so I won't fall

You shade the hottest of days, giving me rest, drink of water
Cool wind upon my face in autumn, you will never falter

Rain upon my roof in spring, showers upon the pavement
Long rides along the countryside, you're the forever fragrance

You do not yell nor scream, you're directly to the point
Encouraging me always to move forward, you're omnipotent

I'm never alone in the dark; the light can never be diminished
For you're always by my side, and for this I will not relinquish

I must now die to myself; fully take on the eternal Truth
Putting on the armor you provide, once given in my youth

For your words I hold onto, close to my heart for protection
They shield me from the storm, and from being sectioned

So now I release my heart to you, singing songs of praise
For you are my past, my present, and all my future days

Silence Is Our Enemy

July 24, 2017

The crowds start to vanish, the quiet fills the empty space
The rains start to fall gently, times running out in the race

My heart sometimes heavy, these eyes are getting old
My youth escapes my body, I'm scared and lonely, I fold

Bitterness creeps into my life, regrets of plenty pass my mind
Have I wasted all these years being idle? Questions I find

Answers I've evaded for the Truth slips through my fingers
If I only took the time to see, sadly on the past I linger

Never in the moment, sickness falling upon my shoulders
Forgetting all that should matter, family weighing like boulders

My blood runs thick as thieves, she lays alone tonight in tears
I've abandoned her into the pits of Hell, for too many years

Silence is both our enemy, miles stretch us so very far apart
Her lies add up and multiply, hard and saddened is her heart

She only has pictures now, children, family, no one trusts!
Caught up in scandal, years oversexed, poisoned, and lust

She will die this way, alone with no one at her bedside
It hurts so much to say, but there's no doubt, she can't hide

My prayers fall short, I'm distracted, put everything on hold
Contemplating whether to call, the situation is out of control

We pretend it's mere illusion, it will fade away in the end
One day disappearing into the abyss, never to be seen again

My mind on overload, these cuts run deep, I bleed heavy
These nightmares never seem go away, I don't feel I am ready

The screen no longer keeps my attention, I now despise
It sickens my soul to watch death, the insanity and lies

I'm afraid of disappointing, letting down the whole race
Falling behind the pack, ashamed of myself, my own face

These days have been dark, these nights have been long
Weeks turn into months, keep on asking is it right or wrong

I'm tired of deception; I look for something to hold onto
An object of love, ignorance and blindness are not virtue

Pleasures are overrated; all I ever want is to be missed
Thinking of me when I'm not around, someone to kiss

Affection eludes me, feel I'm being set of for failure
It's a story that last a lifetime, I feel I have failed her

I always say I'm sorry, I didn't mean what I had said
I cringe at my weaknesses, I have nowhere to rest my head

Please help me, Lord, is my final prayer today and tonight
For at times I feel I'm losing the battle, I'm losing the fight

Please come now, my time has stopped, I have run dry
This is my shout out to heaven: take them, Lord, let them fly!

I've Got Nothing

July 27, 2017

In between the lines, collecting dust, dying bones are crying out
Beginning to the end, rusted roots gathering
the earth all round about

Life fading with each passing moment, nothing really making sense
In relevance to the universe spinning, all through God's lenses

Questions lead to uncertainty, losing hope, all fades in the moment
Rationality springs forth illusion, mistakes
plenty, we all fail to own it

Stones crumble gathering to piles of corruption, his withered hands
Axe to the grind, days blistering hot, desert storms of fine sands

Like molding clay and sword, blazed in the fires of its creator
Shaped and formed into a new version, once formless as a crater

The potter, the field to the plow, hunting the lands of our fathers
Gathering the grain and fruits, our sickened earth is now devoured

Trickling waters polluted by the toxins of
our human corrupted minds
Escaping earth's atmosphere by vehicle, sonic bomb to never find

A farce, a lie, man's manipulation, arrogance to escape the inevitable
Brainwashed by one, a plan set forth, agencies that are inequitable

Sour grapes spoiled by time, wastelands infested by possession
Overspending and buying, accumulating
wealth without any question

Programs funded by the commoner, exterminating all loose ends
What they call progression and science, while calling us their friends

Hammer to nail, mason molding stone,
fire cooking, roof for protection
Though they may not be calamities, they all exist by man's selection

Moving forward through space ever so dark, expanding beyond view
Looking through the looking glass so narrow, our vision lead askew

Wars of darkness spewed forth from the
bowels of hell, bombs launch
Technology brings the end of time; our
sins of playing god are botched

Seed left by the waist side devoured by the serpent, gnashing teeth
Scorning, mocking, grinning he smiles, belly cold from underneath

Vanishing act, the actors are dead, their
silhouettes pass by the screen
Dead photographs, emptiness inside, their
pleasure filled in every scene

The cancer embodies his soul; the sickness
takes the mind overwhelming
Escape was the intent, it's out of control,
into the filth he has now fell in

Overdrive and overload, mind races with
no end in sight filled with rage
Seconds, hours, days, upon years, locked up like a lion in his cage

Pacing, filled with anxiety, prescriptions
filled to the max take the vein
Thoughts fill his mind; paranoia takes
control, losing all of what was sane

She's locked up once more, regret's her
only friend, hasn't called in days
Nights spent in solitude, screaming from
within, she's shredded and frayed

Steel cold to the touch, hell spills over her
shaken body sweat and tears
Nothing left to blame, her children now gone, all these wasted years

Ink spills on the page, thoughts race, ideas
scattered filling the canvas
Dampness fills the midsummer air, the
beast in the night runs rampant

Regrets and sorrow is their only friend,
waiting for the return of the king
Tribulation is in this moment lasting what
seems eternity ruled by the ring

One belly filled with nourishment, one filled with poison and terror
Ripping her body to certain shambles,
selling her soul, heart now severed

The exchange is simple, new life, and new
beginning, just give me your spirit
Tell me all you know, false promises of
yesteryear, ecstasy, you'll feel it

Ranting, abruptly his thoughts scatter,
thinking of when he was a boy
His faith was his strength, laughter so
simple and pure for he was coy

Looking into dead eyes, predators in and out of the children's lives
Left to fend for themselves day after day,
stabbed and cut with the knives

Closet filled with papers, scattered dreams
of a child, growing up too fast
He can't give her anything, he was selfish, and
this moment wasn't meant to last

Her days filled with rage, innocence in exchange for a piece of bread
Turning a blind eye, forgetting family,
both father and son now dead

The plan was for this very moment empty,
apathy and empathy gone
Chartered and mapped out for thousands
of years, this is my fight song

He falls asleep at the wheel all too often;
water is now his only choice
Looking for a way out he runs to the finish
line, his heart is his only voice

Sounds of the night blend and bleed into
the early hours of the morning
City lights in the distance glow, the ache
and pain inside, he's conforming

Becoming what they want, an outlet, and
spark put to gasoline, burst to flame
Another drug to consume, another death
added to the list of the insane

Trust is the issue, eyes so condescending,
calling out your every word
Behind your back speaking ill you laughing,
as the milk sours and curds

His friends cold blooded, their intent is
wicked, and their insanity is their gift
Blinded he's lead into the desert giving
over his friend, like wheat is sift

False promises, lonely hearts, emptiness
feeding the hunger deep inside
Heaven so close, seems out of reach, all
these nights alone he has cried

Years filling the pillow with tears, face down
upon the pillow he screamed
Blessing ignored, shame his only companion,
nightmares to dark dreams

Anguish and misery, demons created
within his mind, he's the puppet
Strings lead his movements, day to day
being led astray, trying to forget it

For the tale started long ago and there's nothing left to say or to do
I've got nothing my dear old friend, we've
all been deceived, but we're the few

Sex Slaves

July 30–31, 2017

The eyes of the elite watch over young skin, tender soft
Soulless eyes, emptiness inside, minds of filth and of rot

Gather together to acclaim their pleasure, the sickness is fed
Rapping innocence striped of their youth, all shame left instead

Sold into slavery, families having nothing, for a piece of bread
Told they'll be safe, treated like kings and queens they said!

They say power and money cannot be touched, cycle continues
Everyone has a price, no one will talk; there are no rules

Demons are what they are, their obsession is most twisted
Sifting out the light within, stealing all their talents gifted

The young grow old, joy, laughter here today and gone tomorrow
The child left asking why? All they feel now is certain sorrow

We're used, bought, and sold, the price tag is most inundate
The cycle repeats itself throughout the ages and is most abundant

Is there no end? Is there a cure? Only time can play this out
God will not watch on forever, His furry one day will no doubt

His wrath and vengeance will prevail; the truth will be a sword
Kings, queens, governors, senators, lobbyists, all in accord

Families at the top of the chain sit round the table of corruption
We're mocked as they laugh filling their bellies full of seduction

Perverseness of their mind control, bodies mortal and corrupted
An island of desire, self-discipline is a myth, youth abducted

Kiss and I will not tell, a pact made by predators in this cult
Covered up behind the scenes, the deceiver's presence is felt

What is your pleasure? What are your needs? Is this what you wish?
Stars tonight fall from the heavens, as the money dockets up the list

Molestation devours this generation's future, eyes blankly stare
They're forged in the stench of the bowels of Hell, playing unfair

Fornication, lust of adolescence is their god, rituals of their delight
Hidden in the shadows behind the scenes, in the darkness, no light

You cannot hide from the Truth, your plan may be in full effect
Though the war is in its final stages, and now the liars will now elect

A prince of darkness, a thief, deceiver, promises empty, no substance
Nothing to lean on but a farce, a coward, sex appeal his resemblance

The top of the food chain eat the poor, vomit them, we ask for mercy
Nothing changes, their power increases, their gods are their furry

Having no allies, self-indulgences beyond measure, without justice
Their end is drawing near, though we may stagger, God has called us

The chosen know the debauchery; we have seen the work at hand
Their castles fill the earthly realm, building their mansions in the sand

The smell of death fills the sickened air they breathe looking to seduce
They kept their names, we've lost our identity; we have been reduced

Now is the time to open our eyes, the chest board is set, make a move
As sure as the sunsets in the west, we must stay awake and not aloof

Dark Matter

June 25, 2017

Seed of dark angels, intermingling with our kind
Raging waters from the abyss, these are the signs

Coming into existence, burning with smoldering flame
Rotting smells of waste, the blood splatters and stains

Witt, charm, and deceit, upon his lips and his tongue
Eyes most cunning, words torch and burn like the sun

Relief with cool wind and rains, nowhere in our sight
Days blackened without hope, no stars to light the night

Promises are empty, glasses filled with blood of death
Deranged and mangled with distort are all that's left

Fear amongst the citizens, anxiety beyond compare
Legions of sour grapes, faces come, go, blankly stare

Like soldiers marching in sync, to destiny in-between
Grey nor black or white tell the story never seen

His thoughts conduct the band, no ally or true friend
For wickedness rules his world, error he now sends

Mistakes multiplied by thousands, no original thought
Sickness fills his days so cold, mind is filled with rot

Furry and rage cross the skies, polluting our fallen world
Warriors without question, ponder thoughts turn, swirl

Dropping to their doom, trampled underfoot like waste
Begging for mercy without pain, praying for death to taste

Torment fills our space and time, the clock ceases to exist
Our days are now numbered few, the years are now fixed

Portholes spewing fire without life, racing down to earth
Upon the speed of light without haste we now await the birth

The age of demise, the age of regret, the age of deception
Sex and lust are his weapons, symbols of his corruption

They walk amongst us, look around you and you'll see
A wink, a whisper, a false promise, you will wish to flee

Appealing to all the masses, both old and young alike
To buy or sell come through him, whether wrong or right

One ring to rule them all, government feeds the poor
Lost souls and minds clutter, waiting for what's in store

Collaboration of past ideas, brought together all in one
Leaders of our history united all together to and from

The banquet table is set, though none of it is for us to eat
For gluttony is his only friend, the table only has one seat

Past wars tear bodies to shreds, this one tears apart souls
We'll soon pray for bullets, we'll be flocking to the polls

Placing him as guest of honor, rolling out the red carpet
The dawn seems so far away, he is as filthy as the harlot

No rules, no trust, nothing pure or innocent fill the halls
Only souls to feed on, vanity, sin of plenty is his call

Please take this as warning, for the days are few in number
Stay awake and wait patiently, stay sober, do not slumber

My Escape

June 26, 2017

My escape is my pen, my options limited to one
Though hate and fear may consume, I will not run

His design we cannot ignore, we cannot deny
His love and passion are immense, he cannot lie

I lean upon my Savior; I look to heaven with praise
My attitudes will not falter, nor his eternity of days

Though my concentration wonders, his heart I seek
At times I want to run and hide, my soul is most weak

Narrow my mind cannot comprehend his salvation
His understand beyond compare without mention

I feed upon his promises of eternal life with much pleasure
Fighting through the darkest of days and nights I endeavor

Bliss, love, passion and grace is enough to get me through
For all my very existence I have been free because of you

Decisions and crossroads and splits, where to go I pray
This bed I have made this morning, last throughout the day

Upon my pillow I lay my head; I look to heaven with hope
Counting all my blessings I receive, the patience to cope

My own will is not enough; my own thoughts seem to fail
With your intercession I will succeed, into sunsets I sail

Saints of heaven intercede, requesting my second chance
Without their constant prayer, I couldn't make a stance

To the east I watch life rise, to the west I find your color
Bright pinks, purples, and blues of awe there is no other

To hear nature sing out with praise, skies filled with song
To see fields of green pasture, your creation there's no wrong

Though we fail to see your face, from day to day most sad
In your arms I'm safe and sound, your passion not a fade

Phases are mere illusion; your time can not be measured
Gratification of this life are found in your eyes with pleasure

No earthly food or drink, could ever replenish soul or mind
For upon your shoulders the world rest, we will surely find

Though these earthly days are shortened and numbered
Our tears are wiped away by grace, I will never slumber

Though frail and fragile are my ways, the path is straightened
You never left me even I my doubt, you never have forsaken

My mind is fixed upon you; the future is in your hands
My faith is in every step I take, you have counted of the sands

You know the hairs upon my head, the prayer upon my heart
You know where I've been, you've been there since the start

You've walk upon the water, ways are beyond comprehension
I will never doubt again, you saved my life I'll forever mention

Heaven's Light

April 15, 2017

Rising sun brings forth anticipation, day bleeds with delay
Waiting, patience crashing down, counting the minutes away

You radiate with Heaven's light, a gem, diamond in the rough
An Angel could not compare, I could never write enough

My words fail me at this moment, a poem or song couldn't do
For description of your being is beyond earthly words I have for you

Walking by your side, through forest thick with sounds of delight
Peering into your green eyes, you give me reason, hope, and fight

I see your gentle soul, I hear you speak words with great strength
I watch you walk with Grace, going the extra mile and length

Your poised, intellectual, beauty beyond measure, none compare
Uniqueness is what separates you; you're righteous and most fair

A prayer is an understatement; you're an answer to a call
Sharp minded and witty, my knees bend every moment and I fall

Days and nights echo into the abyss, you stay firm and bold
The sun shines upon your fields, rain quenching thirst, I fold

My cards and bet are on you, stars burn
with purpose and command
God's plan included you from the start, our final fight and stand

Release your heartache; release your doubt and all of your fears
Regain the passion within, the hurt inside, I can catch your tears

Possessions accumulate over time, but friendships last forever
Won't you put your hand in mine? I must make this endeavor

Fortitude is a given, I would wait till the end of time if I must
One would be a fool to let you go, but I am one you can trust

I'll listen so intently, you can lean on me when you're weary
I'll be there at the gate lending my hand, you mustn't be leery

You make me smile, you make me quiver, make my knees weak
You make me come back for more, your knowledge I seek

Your face burns within my thoughts; your voice calms my soul
Your smile is a mystery, through all pressure you advance in control

Taking the long way home, taking in the scenery all around
Breathing in the air on a summer's night with the windows down

Touching the cool night breeze, taking in all the sights and sounds
I could listen to for eternity, me, I was once lost and now I found

Colors painted on a canvas couldn't do any justice or decree
For when you walk in a room heads turn, if not they cannot see

My eyes are open to your heart; it beats with life and desire
Flames bursting all around, one would be either a fool or liar

If he couldn't take notice to your truth, overflowing with rapture
They would be lost without hope, one could never again capture

Watching you dance and sing, seeing your eyes lock with mine
Simple things you do that make me smile
knowing everything is fine

Fire in His Eyes

September 11, 2017

He's coming from the clouds on high, descending like a dove
He comes with fire in his eyes ragging, in a furry of pure love

With a sword in his mouth, and with passion by his waist
He comes with an army of angels, our sins we must face

To heaven we will be plucked up, most will be left behind
The war has been fought and won, he comes with a sign

The cross isn't just a symbol; it is what saved us from hell
His torture wasn't in vain; it is ever lasting water from the well

His pouring of self is our inheritance, though we are weak
The blood and water from his side, his power I surely seek

He comes down to strike the head of the snake, wars complete
On his throne he ever reigns on high, I now pray for a seat

At the banquet table, I truly wish to always be by his side
Eternity Father, Son, Holy Spirit in one; darkness can't hide

For the light will not be foreshadowed, we will surely see
The King will rule forever, from the greatest down to me

These days have now been shortened, though time numbered
He has made this night great, we mustn't walk in a slumber

I see him on the mountain tops, in the clouds, and in the mist
I see him in a baby's eyes, I could go on forever with a list

The mother has cried many nights, wishing her babe well
The mother has cried many days, counting teardrops that fell

Fallen to the ground, salt in the wound, enemies on all sides
The devil is now lashing out one last time, wailing he cries

Shouting out, shaking fist to the heavens, fire he will burn
The Spirit soon will descend upon the advocate, wheels churn

Spinning the coil, reaction for all actions, consequences return
The final days have approached, like a thief guilty will burn

Sentenced to death, for repentance was far from the intentions
Denial of the truth will be costly, what is in store I mention

For I heed this final warning, fire and brimstone will rain down
The ground will shake, hail fire, starvation, grinding teeth sound

They'll be nowhere to hide, the trumpets will be blown loud
The division of the chosen and damned, humble from the proud

Pride has killed many, brought forth prisoners strong and weak
Our Savior comes shinning; bright armor, he protects the meek

The sounds of the night give way to the morn, breath of fresh air
For he comes while the earth is drunk, all will admire and stare

We are distracted, we are beaten; we are battered and bruised
Sadly we have forgotten we did same to him, we're the accused

We are guilty of our crimes, now he comes amongst the earth
We will truly regret our coming actions, feel the pains of birth

This day soon shall come to close, this plea heard on deaf ears
For we're sadly sickened with lies, we all give into the fear

For when I wake up in the morn, the truth I shall give to all
These final days of numbered down to the second, I hear the call

Her Body in Shambles

September 13, 2017

Inferior is the body and the tissue, failing in tests over time
For the skin peels and burns, to not forgive is my only crime

Uneasy is the silent night; winds blow stale and dull, envious
With jealousy I peer into the privileged eyes, I'm delirious

Insanity is what keeps me from falling this night, head afloat
The waters are raging, seas arise; I've bottomed out so low

I speak like a child coiled up, naked amongst the crowd still
My voice lost in the echo, searching for numbness, a pill

Excuses is all I have left, time seems against me in the fight
My silence is my own worst enemy, losing all hope and sight

Idleness takes the call, unprepared and lazy, talents wasted
The pages whisper the words low, victories he's never tasted

Unprepared nights of rehearsal, timid manner, yoke is heavy
For the burden he places upon his shoulder, breaking the levy

Drowning amongst the waters, stagnant, quench not my thirst
For the arid, empty, vast desert destroys all life, I feel cursed

My blessings I fail to count, for the other side is most tempting
The grass seems greener; more lush, wish to own, not renting

Buying time is what seems to be my foe, another day passes by
Another dollar goes to waste, uncharitable heart filled with lies

Deceit, twisting truths slowly like a mountain unwinding slow
The still of the eve is ruthless; unsteady my hands and the flow

My father sleeps sound tonight, buying his right to rest his head
Worries drift away for daily pressures; she lay there instead

Cage made of steel, walls cold to the touch, screams in her mind
Her life is a lie, she cries wolf, her actions and ways are the signs

All these years on this planet have been overshadowed by the dark
The light within me has seemed to vanish, I wish for just a spark

Reflections amongst the still water mirrors, reflecting the sun
The stars dimmed out by man, my heart dimmed out, now I run

Avoiding the problem with false solution, blending in with crowd
Heart races, blood boils, losing all control, screaming all around

The families collide like matter upon antimatter coming together
The results catastrophic, can anything positive result, I'm weathered

The dark rest their heads comfortable
tonight, rest from strong drink
Drink and toast to our misfortune from our pains, to when we sink

Art spilled forth by painting, pictures depicting words unspoken
Its true form a thing of beauty and taste,
showing man's heart broken

Art written in story, both fiction and in truth, giving us warning
Painting images seared in our minds, from
our past mistakes learning

The dilemma now is the art; they have ripped my sister's soul apart
They have beaten, tortured, and rapped
her; this my friend is not art

I'll never understand her pain, the cancer that lives inside of her
She is filled with death, her body is desecrated; nights are obscure

Desperate measures taken, whirlwind takes her moments by storm
Calling devils to align, unit, impossible;
for there is no sense or norm

Chaos, insanity captures every moment like a still frame, frozen
The sickness takes their mind and vein;
punctured in rooms they're in

For the wounds no longer find themselves, but their families, friends
Images in his mind of yesterday, could he have given a hand to lend?

The day, the night, the year begins; terror now consumes her being
Though poison slips out her body, the truth she fails to be seeing

Trust

September 14, 2017

Trust is a word born from the darkness, brought forth into light
It's malleable, transformed, and molded, giving us sight

Bursting from the flames forged, blindly bonding two or more
Trust is more than a mere word; it has formed kingdoms of score

Trust is taking a leap in faith, knowing you'll fall safe and sound
Giving yourself to another, two becoming one and are bound

Combining knowledge and wisdom, using discernment from both
Realizing not just knowing, acceptance of another, not to loath

It tolerates differences of opinion, yet justifies only truth
It extends verily from the elder, in between, and our youth

Trust brought forth treaties, peace, promises of better tomorrows
It sets forth journeys of great distance, has both pity and sorrow

Forgiveness for our male intent, our shortcomings, and failures
Trust is a shot in the dark made by faith, the fruit of our labor

Not knowing you'll receive recompense, payment, reconciliation
Placing all of your eggs in one basket, it has no frustration

It will never come back without void, for the receiver embraces
The bond yet not physical, wed in heaven, it's free not in cages

Trust is the hidden link, the key, the porthole of our universe
It never screams or shouts, it has only courage and doesn't curse

Its rules are just a given, bound by common courtesy and sense
It doesn't beat around the bush, it sees clearly through the lens

Sharp and keen is its sight, never missing the target or the mark
Trust is never flipping a coin, it's always to the point; it's stark

It's knowing I'll get up in the morning, knowing you'll be there
It's always been there in your eyes, for I've found it in you stare

For if you ever doubt me in this life, just remember this rhyme
It's because of whom you are I trust, I know forever I'll be fine

Sun Fades West

September 17, 2017

Searching for a moment divine, light years beyond our view
Finding a diamond in the rough, all along it had been you

I found true love when I wasn't looking; I struck me to the core
My heart once hardened and cold, knew now what this life is for

My weakened knees, my loss of breath, the ache in my throat
Every time I drew you near, kept me from drowning, staying afloat

That kiss near your mailbox; those nights beneath the stars above
The moments listening to music, your pure smile, radiating love

Watching you play guitar, your hair in your face, green eyes
Your fair skin and freckles, hand and hand, you never told lies

The nights and days on the train, car rides, looking into your soul
Holding you in my arms so true, the day you left I felt so low

The drawings you made for me, the letters, pictures I held so close
Memories I'll never forget, the heart made of wood, color rose

Nights staying up till sunrise, talking endlessly, hand and hand
Our first time at the beach together, catching rays upon the sand

The times next to the fire, watching fireflies in the summer sky
The fires ash rising above us, moments like this you can't buy

Burning CD's, Matchbox Twenty, Dave Matthews, and more
Concerts, getting Celtics tickets, buying crafts together at the store

Making T-shirts, apple club, days spent just being, hanging out
You getting stung by that bee, getting lost amongst the crowd

Summer nights spent with friends, the whispering in my ear
The secrets told between us will cherish, with you I had no fear

Across a land so fast you reside, mountains, valleys, rivers long
Fields of gold, crops so lush, plains, with you I can't go wrong

The rushing calm waters at bay, peace, tranquil, pass by with force
Now the city embraces your moments, while I'm in a maze, a course

Trying to break through the mold of society, becoming a man
A person I was meant to be, oceans crossed through seas to land

I found it in your eyes, your grace, your lips so soft, tender sweet
I discovered it in your touch, without you there's an empty seat

A seat seeming impossible to fill, a chair sits across this lonely room
Staring back at me in disgust, I'm in constant solitude in my tomb

A grave I dug myself, though some would say it's been too long
Far too long to hold onto still, I must let
go, and right out the wrong

You're seared within my consciousness all time, angels face indeed
I'm haunted by your absence, wondering where my days will lead

The night has cancelled out and bled today, another day has passed
Without you there by my side I withdraw, these moments never last

For they're gone, swiftly tossed into the
breeze, lost in the sea of time
The perfect love seems so distant, they'll never be another or kind

You're the first and last to hold my hand dear, I never will forget
For you'll always be my love, for the sun chases you into the west

Before the Light

September 19, 2017

Before the light, darkness covered the land, the land was at peace
Nothing, stillness filled the soundless sky, calming solitude

The shifts, the movements, undisturbed, untouched, erythematic
All the features in the world before light, the light would bring day

Days would conquer over the darkness,
light bringing forth knowledge
Wisdom, answers, complication set forth, the prince would ponder

Devising plans to destroy creation, the darkness once held dominion
A strangle hold over the light, blocking out the toxic rays, blinding

The prince would wait, gather his angels, scheming, conjuring
The light would bring forth image, sight would open our eyes

Our eyes would be easily deceived by the light, darkness covers
My eyes are seared by the unveiling of
his plan, the prince in shadow

Shadows hide the image set forth by the light, I hide, I'm in fear
Constant terror fills my days; not wanting
to sin, yet the light finds me

She dances by the light, the prince half
grin smile, watches me; mocks
My peace is my solitude in the darkness,
darkness is where I progress

My eyes are shut to the lusts of this life,
the prince gathers knowledge
I am weak, my skin burns in the light, my flesh is weak, corruption

Decaying body made to be destroyed by the light, I sit in darkness
I cry out in the desert, shouting to heaven
above for answers, I'm alone

Alone in a world where image rules,
violence, sex, hate; the light shines
In darkness nothing can be seen, nothing
can be contrived, emptiness

A vast sea of darkness fills my being; I feel
no pull, no rebellion for once
Light brings forth the beast, his prince shows me ungodly images

Images burned into my nights and days
because of the light, unsettling
Cancerous is the rays of the light, the prince brings forth deception

I am deceived because the light betrays my
eyes, darkness my innocence
Innocence ripped from me, I've been
raped by the light, never healed

I wish now to leave this world, the light has caused too much pain
We lust over the light, we sin over the light, I have taken advantage

I am cursed because of the light, my eyes
I seem not to control, misery
The light brought forth war, it brought forth
lies, and it brought forth shame

My shame I cannot hide, I search for
solitude in the darkness, lifeless
My body aches for time changes, my promises I do not keep, I lie

For the light causes me to form and mold,
bonds broken, disorientation
Life here would seize to exist without the light, I survive by darkness

Though nature takes in the light, it to
dies, it is destroyed by the cycle
In the darkness I cannot see the dancing silhouettes, the dark prince

He displays the images for all to see, I am
part of the problem, the light
I was once in the darkness, innocent, unknown, avoiding psychosis

I am sick because of the light, my tears my
only companion, in darkness
For the darkness blocks out the images of terror; terror fills my days

The prince brought forth the light, though
his time soon comes to pass
No longer will neither the darkness nor
light rule, but heavens kingdom

I See Your Face

September 20, 2017

I see your face; it shines forth amidst the sun, moonlit sky
Radiant in color, white light unimaginable, painting in motion

Telling parables of wisdom, hinting clues of what to come
The night wind goes forth without asking, rain beating down

The mount on the temple, veil torn in two, earth swallows up
Long winding paths through the streets, heavy and burdensome

Details of your face, pressed image, blood impression on cloth
Sermons, beauty from your lips, the seas rough with waves

I see your face, your eyes in the night, looking back in mirror
Reflections so imperfect, calling out quietly, shivering cold rain

Your eyes pierce me, cut my breath short, I ignore your call
Speaking to me in the eve frantically, falling fast into your arms

Water to wine, lame cured, the dead raised to life, miracles
Miracles go unseen to our eyes each day, baby is born, soul given

Old man, passerby on the street, begging for change, for bread
Woman all used up, beaten, battered, waiting for her end to come

These are your children, our children, the young grow old sadly
Cain to Abel, shattering blows, up close and personal, kill shot

Our youth intentionally lied to, led astray, askew, into the desert
His eyes saddened, our intelligence misleads us and our values

Wise man forgotten, tossed aside, water to wine, miracle ignored
Man made by God, in the beginning was the word, word made flesh

I hear their laughter, their soul lights a spark in my eyes, silence
Days spent with disciples, laughing, learning, tossing waves in night

Walking on water yet again ignored, fables and tails, fabrication
Explained, hypothesis, scientific facts conjured, taken as fact, lies

I see your face, weathered, your soul pure, radical your actions
Curing the insane with your command, spit and dirt cleansing eyes

I'm hungry for your return, a king wrapped in majesty, we wait
Tribulation marks my days, getting lost in the confusion, trials

Table set for a king, humble, breaking bread, your body and blood
Man tossing aside as symbolism, spitting in your face once again

The night grows cold and damp, morning just on the horizon
The song calls me, the hunger presses me on; a new year begins

Signs of the seasons set in the stars, constellations in the night sky
Your command of a room immense, unimaginable presence felt

Child sees his mother with care, disciplined, taught by scholars
A system now set up by fascist, we're ants marching to the furnace

Thoughts impede his progression, the cross road is close at hand
Your body wrapped in cloth, blood stained, gently placed in tomb

A church made of men, sin, threatening our values, truth hidden
Self-centered ego maniacs, answering to an unknown name above

The list of families set forth, the bloodlines, documented by man
Family trees planed out overtime, intertwining, intermingling

The shadows, the thorns, the thickets grown to choke out life
Yet I see your face radiant, shinning forth with bright color beauty

The garden where you knelt, praying, your cup I could not bear
My body aches with a pain minor in comparison, my mind sick

The man looking back at me in disgust, the mirror picks me apart
I long for truth, not to be vain, crushing the head of the serpent

They've known just what to do; the plan was set forth over time
Old man at my door; middle of the night, his eyes, laugh deceiving

Winds grow furious, the choir shouts in unison, the battle continues
This day brought forth, approaches on schedule, shadows linger

Illusions fill the blank pages, the book written with false pretense
The true book written with proven accuracy, all perfect his ways

Your face I see trying to hide, your light immense shining brightly
I am the prodigal son, I am Judas, I am the betrayer; I am saved

I am part of the few chosen; my line will not be erased, forgotten
This child is cold, thought this child is not forgotten, I see your face

Spider's Web

September 21, 2017

Season ends, rushing winds howl throughout the last summer eve
Spider web intrinsically made with precision,
he is one with the weave

Destruction in the south amounts, natural disasters accumulating
As I sit here safe, caught up in the chaos,
turmoil, and my frustration

Relativity is a hand, my sickness, their misery linked together
Nature continues to rebuild without complaint, flight of the feather

Storms violently toss the waves, the earth
shakes violently tearing apart
Forces of nature never seen before, I reside in tranquility, written art

Language painting the canvas, layer after layer telling a story of new
Old tales replenishing our stubborn viewpoint,
unwinding mountain view

It to moves over time, as we stick here relevantly speaking, frozen
As motionless in the mountain in our
conquests, our lives are interwoven

The spider waits, anticipation without
anxiety, the prey falls into the trap
Our lives so similar in comparison, we
disregard each other, we overlap

Thrown to the wolves, tossed to the sharks,
blood poured into the water
The cycle continues, though we have
rationality and reason, we falter

Days are now shortened, still the winds
are reversed, time only will tell
The secret plan will shortly be revealed, the greedy soon will sell

For the pawns will suffer great lose, falling fast into the web of lies
My friend we have been warned, we now
face our fate, look to the sky

The telling of the seasons, the moon, the
sun, the painting tells the story
The note is in his hands, he sits in the
chair; we're redeemed by his glory

The night rings out the telling sign of
autumn, leaves changing color
I sit here in solitude awaiting the change,
I'm not alone, there's another

The race approaches without hesitation,
the day holds somber, I'm tired
Weary soul looks above, eyes fixated on the cross, for he is not a liar

Poison fills my veins tonight, as in the morn I start new once again
For the dosage changes as prescribed, my
canvas and page, my friend

Excitement avails my days, no longer do
I seek pleasure without fantasy
I'm stuck in one place, under the mountain
deep, stuck under the canopy

The destructive path of the storm I desire, I would gladly embrace
For my days are overwhelming, fearful, lined with rot and are laced

I face the moments, looking them in the
eye, knowing my enemy is near
For he knows our weakness's, he's in this room watching also in fear

Anxiety races, the pace is quickened, the
finish line seems out of reach
Both him and I know all too well the end
is near, though he is the leech

For the change of season is at hand, the year's final cycle comes forth
Autumn begins at once, winter approaches
methodically from the north

The winds change course according to our Lord's wishes from above
For his language is purity, his sword is
sharp, ways encompassing love

New World Order

July 15, 2017

A watchful eye is upon us, separating the elite from the weak
Blacks, whites, Hispanics, are grouped, vengeance they seek

Divisions the goal, false flags the key, morality is now lost
His time is running out, furry now His weapon, lives the cost

The Order is in place, the plan set for all the ages of the past
Time has now have grown silent, the masses are tossed and cast

The classes have been torn apart, the poor multiply and suffer
Government grows immensely; the silent enemy is under cover

Freedom traded in for protection, we're nursed from the bottle
Poison's in the water, drugs given to our children we're coddled

Our vote is a farce, the goal is to destroy, give illusions of hope
In private they laugh, hanging the poor from the noose by a rope

The media tells lies; false flags ravage the wires of the outlets
Movies, television, internet, paper blood, images of fake conquest

Civilian clothes worn by both the enemy
and our soldiers on the field
Who is to blame is the question, the crop is now ready to be wield

Ignorance of our youth are sucked into battle, losing all dignity
Promises of a better future they're deceived, they're lost for eternity

Destroyed limbs, destroyed minds, destroyed families ripped apart
For the agenda of the elite is twisted, and has been from the start

Promises of health care, welfare, social security, government checks
We're Promised Land and opportunity;
we're slaves, certainly wrecked

We're told to point the finger, they are
the ones, and they are to blame
My friend, look from within, there lies the answer, we're all the same

Are soldiers are sent around the world,
policing almost every country
Protecting opium fields without question,
all for we call blood money

Women serve to fight wars of horror, instead of the war of Heaven
Fighting in Satan's army, instead of being
care bearers of our children

A woman's body is a vessel of hope, life, and future of our kind
Sacred is her gifts, protection is a man's gift to her like the vine

The vine representing our families over space and over time
Fighting at the front lines for their integrity,
upon the cross is his sign

The fight between the sexes, the battle for what we call equality
Falsified by lies and deceit, the argument
with holes and is most faulty

Is there collusion with the enemy? Is war
the only answer now upon us?
Has the goal been this from the beginning? The deceiver now cusses!

Bombs, ammunition, tanks, guns are out
of the equation and solution
Now drones fill the sky with fear, with manipulation and pollution

Genocide of plenty fills our homes with lies, killing children, infants
We call it protection, contraception, we're blind without deliverance

Laws were made to serve and protect, they were limited and simple
Years went by, money was to be made, and
then there became a wrinkle

Law upon a law, and exception to an exception, lost in translation
Followed by misleading the witness, with illusion and exaggeration

Jobs lost overseas to save government notes, avoiding taxes and fees
Machines to take over labor, computers to crunch numbers and lean

False prophets promising the world, images of sex, material things
Lobbyist within government, granting wishes, even golden rings

A ring to rule the multitudes, world government,
and the masses suppressed
With elegant tone they speak, convincing even the wise to confess

Giving up their rights, freedoms to live
and provide for their families
The outer beauty of a model is democracy
now and sadly the assembly

Our children have been attacked, left wing
education system is emplaced
Fascism is now the model, their minds and freewill have been erased

Told to make a stance, stand up for what you
think is right, everything is gray
Told there is no black and white, we're told
to live for tomorrow not today

The rainbow generation is here, goodbye
to generation X and beyond
Everyone is suspicious, guilty before proven
innocent, what has gone wrong?

The jobs have been limited, health care,
education, some but very few
Others include lawyers, doctors, and retail, we sell nothing, it is rue

We produce close to nothing; we only resell
what has already been made
We make alcohol, cigarettes, and
pornography while our morals fade

Better yet now we legalize marijuana, same
sex marriage; it is our right!
Here no one's right or wrong, seems whatever
you feel is your true sight!

Woman getting gang raped, beaten bruised
crushed, left to die and suffer
While the silent killers laugh and mock,
dignity gone as they taunt her

The drug wars are pushed, they never even really cared much at all
As the needle takes the vein of our teens,
another dies in a bathroom stall

We pick and choose the timing of everything,
we pretend we are Gods
When to have children choosing how many
and when, the Creator we forgot

Wars fought over bonds, keeping the value of our dollar in trade
Put above all other currency on earth,
the value diminishes and fades

A sense of security permeates throughout
our blind society so sickening
Walls could not hold back the enemy,
feels as if we have been forsaken

The sides have been established, our allies far and few in between
The muscle is our military, seeming now only to be a cruel scheme

BRICKS nations in place, the stock market
can't push the bubble forever
When will it burst, the dollar pushed aside, it can't always endeavor

The zombie apocalypse is upon us and at hand, laziness the norm
As long as our bellies are full, no one really
cares in regards to the storm

Fear used to be torture of the body, now the mind is a certain risk
Mind control is the new game; the media's
false propaganda is on the list

All this goes on as behind the scenes the
elite laugh with much pleasure
His twisted plan is in full effect, nearing
end now, it can't go on forever

I've seen sickness at first hand; I've tasted the pill and swallowed it
I've lost control of my senses at times, and at times I have faltered

I've walked the hallways of the hospital, heard the cries of the poor
I've seen the hopelessness in their eyes, what
their tomorrows have in store

I've been subdued held against my own will;
felt the needle pressed in deep
I've had plenty of sleepless nights awake, looking for pleasure to seek

Medication runs rampant in our society, seems everyone is at risk
You're Bi-Polar! You're schizophrenic!
Depression at the top of the list

Our children don't have a chance, they need medication, they say!
OCD, ADD, and more top the docket, they're broken and frayed

We pledge allegiance to hatred, democracy is so distant in the past
America by plan is on the demise, we're going nowhere real fast

We watch as the athlete battle on the
diamond, ring, arena, and field
We make them out as gods, as they ruin our future crop and yield

Priorities are out of proportion, we pay Hollywood with barrels gold
Models walk the runway; stun the world
with vanity, selling their soul

Distraction is the name of the game; lives are being lost by the score
Millions suffer minute by minute; common
man asking what's this life for?

He mocks God at all cost, forcing all to sell and by in his name
His solutions to everything is upon us, he will soon rise to fame

The times and seasons have been set,
empty solution and false promise
Filling our homes with corruption, our obedience is his only request

In these trials and this Tribulation, he makes
his final stance and beckons
His angles gather in shadows, the fraudulence
of the vote and write-ins

The prideful boast, they laugh from afar, spitting in our Lord's face
Grace and honor avoid them; it's a fight for
their possessions and their race

Wake, my friend, stay alert at all times
even in the late night early morn
For it comes upon us like a thief in the
night, as he mocks and scorns

The dawn and light is now here, the final
stance is now at the doorstep at hand
The war has now begun, battles have been
fought, stay on solid ground, not sand!

Wealth

September 21, 2017

Wealth is knowledge, the truth; information assembled, complete
It's neither gold nor earthly riches, paper notes stacked up neat

Books written recording history; history recorded by sociopaths
With certain agenda, winners chosen by the deceiver's wrath

Swaying the masses to believe anything, evolution of mankind
Single celled organisms forged, blooming to nonsensical design

Wealth is reverse engineering accompanied with original thought
The two coexisting in a bilateral world as one, it cannot be bought

It is priceless, cannot be sold, its memory never ceases to be
Wealth being two steps ahead, never building castles in the sand

It is not relying just on oneself, it's placing all your trust in above
It both using your mind and heart, instincts are never enough

It's witty and wise, it disassembles empires, queens, and kings
For it sees through the darkness, true intent, there's no ending

Wealth is humility, begs only for forgiveness in order to be saved
Knowing your place amongst the ranks, the straight road paved

It's using your head when situations arise, focused upon the now
Anticipating the future with caution, speaking softly never loud

Whispering words that cannot be undone, set solid upon rock
Never takes advantage of the poor, it's the hands on the clock

In sync and aligned with the heavens, formed by a maker divine
Ruled by any debt, no endowment could for fill, it's gentle, kind

Wealth is a tool not to be abused, grows when cultivated with care
Precious stones upon the earth are jealous, they couldn't compare

It exceeds all limits; it rations out its excess, bringing all to table
Forgetting what the commoner owes, releases all fear making stable

Acts of kindness shall not be rendered as weakness, but of love
For wealth of a man is measured in heart, not accumulation of stuff

Time for the great divide has arrived, the table has been set
The uniforms though different in color, all sacredness now has left

The towers have fallen; the knee has dropped in submission
For what we stood first is all forgotten, the
cancer no longer in remission

It is full blown, the final stages, the elite mock us in the shadows
We are all puppets on the string, fitting
our lives meet the status quote

We stand up for the venomous snake; the terrorist is now the idol
For we bow down to the golden calf, the
trigger to the gun we coddle

Money is the motivator, drug money from the pockets of the leaders
The devaluation of the dollar and morality
complete, quarters to the meter

For time has passed away run out, the
wealth of man has spun around
Wealth is no longer charity for another, but blissful ignorance found

History Forgotten

September 26, 2017

Blood seeping into the earth, the mother cries aloud alone
Soldier's torn limb from limb, screaming in horror to come home

Man pretends to know the truths, blames
everyone else for what's wrong
Women on the streets walk as whores, rhythmic beat of tired song

Nothing unique, nothing new, every song and dance done before
The band is synthetic; the lines are dumb downed to lure and lore

Our history has been forgotten; new age
movement has taken center stage
What was once held in high praise now the
villain; the commoner in rage

The flag had shown unity, terrorist blasting
apart buildings declaring war
All is now in the distant past forgotten,
our ignorance settles the score

Bombs bursting in air, what they withstood,
you and I talk on our stool
Our flag was there throughout the night,
now we spit upon it as fools

The pawn sees and his kin now follows suit, oblivious to their stance
Like moths led to the fire to be burned,
never taking a second glance

The divide has come into full effect, leaders sit watching civil war
Blacks versus whites, the rainbow's stance; asking what this life for?

Opinions run rampant, common goal is
lost, baby killers we call them
For once they came back in black bags
from Nam, they can never win

History has repeated itself once again, the
dumb down society watches
Witless our ways as we sleep in anger, our mistakes are so timeless

Never ending, never ceasing, a different
name yet the same old result
Call it left wing, call it right, but in the end they're the same, a cult!

There are no alliances but their own kind,
upper elite pissing upon us
Watching us desecrates the flag and
beyond, our flesh rotting to dust

Are our hero's really in arenas where man
beats upon his fellow man?
Are they in the theater, television screen,
media; castles upon the sand?

Are what they say relevant to us, do they know the mentally insane
Do they know the poor man living by each
paycheck, left out in the rain?

Where does the nonsense end? When does
my grandfather ever get justice?
Standing upon a war ship as a gunner,
facing down the enemy's hit list

The barrel of a gun pointed at the ship,
making its final approach in fear
Men lost at sea and at war upon foreign
lands forever, family left in tears

The goal was to divide and conquer, security
checkpoint, democracy lost
Cameras on every street corner, big brother
watching, freedom's the cost

Are children now defiant, watching
mimicking their idol and their team
Now the priority in our lives is social media,
and the most unique meme

Structure has been lost to chaos, the agent of the Joker and his gang
Chaos now our daily routine, the weatherman's
prediction frame by frame

So please, friend, use your logic, your
reasoning, heart, eyes, and ears
Read, understand their game is to divide;
we mustn't live anymore in fear

Joy in November

November 11, 2016

Joy, laughter, peace, hanging around my atmosphere
No judgment, nothings by mistake is where I found her

The ground under my feet, sometimes shaky at best
The air above me is thick while the sun fades in the west

Freezing air making icicles, snow softly hits her tong
Moon beams hitting her hair glowing like ambers, we run

My fear has had me frozen; sleep had taken over my time
My days are lessened to nothing, holding back all my rhyme

Door closes in anger my nights have been blacken, no light
Until now I have had nothing, within is where I fight

My prayer lifts my head, holding high amongst the trees
The forests of the night stars, once blind now I see

This rope around my neck, these shackles on my feet
Have been tight for too long, I'm restless and I'm weak

My family is my strength; it grows while my years pass by
My friends fade in the background, now asking myself why?

Can't seem to shake the past, my present a prayer in the making
The future is so uncertain, like the morning dew while waking

It fades while the sun beats down, giving clouds to the skies
Returning to the grounds of earth, giving us both wheat and rye

Bread upon our tables, Thanksgiving around our freedoms
Life down from the Cross, once dead, now He leads them

I walk upon the snowfall, His feet in unison by my side
The paths rise and fall sometimes narrow, sometimes wide

This year has been hard, though one thing has been certain
A friend has been forged, a gift from behind the curtain

As Christmas approaches, prayers come back without void
My wish is for His return, pray with aggression being not coy

Plan Continued

August 4, 2017

Plan is to know before hand with foresight,
knowledge, conquer, and defeat
Purpose is having the drive, and motivation,
ambition to move your feet

Everything for His glory is a must; we put him first on a pedestal
Council of His own will, he needs no other,
no one to answer to, no obstacle

Secure and certain are his ways, we shall
not be weary, he knows are fate
Not made by or abandoned the earth, for he's
ever at our side, seasons and dates

Retreat is not an option, we will not back down,
and we stay and fight the good fight
All knowing is his power, he will not be
destroyed, our riches are his delight

Facing hardships is certain, days and nights
heavy, he'll always be by our side
Knowing how is his only path, never a
mistake; let's just hop in for the ride

His kingdom is unshakeable, he's unchangeable,
a force to be reckoned with
His hand moves mountains, shuts the lion's
mouth, the force in which I live

The victory has been won, the war complete,
our salvation attested for
The secret is unveiled for all to see, he came,
he defeated and he conquered

The highest peak and lowest valleys he
reaches, all is in his sight and grasp
For by the very power of the king I latch on,
he's the reason I survive, and last

Though we may be tired or weary, upon
his yoke we may find certain rest
His love is immeasurable beyond all power,
for this fact I firmly can attest

Though at times I may be discouraged, I
look upon his face and plainly see
The man whom burdened sin upon his shoulders,
whom died for both you and me

Though downhearted is my heart in my darkest
of sin, feeling there's no chance
His mercy and grace are sufficient, enough,
for he faces down the demons' stance

I've seen the light, I've seen the darkness, he
has given me the keys, light is there
Now I must open the door for all to see, for
truly Jesus, the King of kings cares

Wishes Fall to Wishes

July 30, 2016

Sitting and waiting for the ship to set and sail away
For comfort is in peace, and patience where I lay

No more phones causing neither chaos, nor media hate
Only the road set before us, watching over my fate

Fear has soaked my bones, much too long the pain
Furry has ripped my soul, my mind at times not sane

The ship has arrived, climbing aboard is what's next
Twisted philosophies collide, where the road connects

The path is long and winding, my eyes raised up high
He looks at me smiling; dark clouds turn to blue skies

I'm forgiven, that's all I need to know now and forever
These days so unforgiving, something I must endeavor

I wait for the fall, the autumn day's coming with chill
For a world less loud, for my destiny to be fore filled

It's time to let go, giving what is certainly true for all
For days that are simple, for days filled with the Call

So as my wishes fall to wishes, and tonight I may feel small
One day I will rise, and in the meantime take the fall

The Stairs

April 28, 2016

I kneeled up high on the stairs, climbing to our Lord up upon the
Cross
Tears flowing endless like a river, the sign I saw up high above two
Hawks

I run growing weary and tired, but His hands hold up my dreary soul
The Saints and Angels sing aloud, now I know I was never the one
in control

I pray to Our Mother above, her heart pure with love never lashing
out
She cries with me begging and pleading, knowing truly what this is
all about

We are saved not because we've earned it, nor do we really even deserve
The plan was designed when time began; my purpose here is only to
serve

My excitement and my Joy come from my child within; he's been
there all along
I find it hiking being one with nature, seeing joy in your eyes, listening to song

I find it taking long walks, swimming in the ocean, feeling the sun
upon my face
I find it talking to the people; it's the feeling when I run for Him and
His Grace

I'm joyful when I write; I'm joyful spending time with friends I truly love
I'm joyful when I watch you laugh so sincere, I'm joyful from the gifts above

To see you dance, talking about your mom and dad, your sister and your friends
I'm even happy when you change your 3 stations, for your broken soul to mend

One day when we reach the other side, my heart will shine bright as the stars
Knowing that your place in Heaven will reach far beyond, healing all your scars

I hope you'll remember me, when you dance with the Angels and I'm in my tent
I hope you'll let me have at least one dance, for now I know why you were sent

You've given me hope, a new perspective; you've given me a second chance
Before you my eyes were blinded, my Sins beyond count, all I needed was a glance

Though the world places me as a failure, I don't have much to give or offer up
My joy is the anticipation of going to Church with you, drinking from the Cup

The Cup of Blood, the Bread His Body, Joy in His voice in scriptures at Mass
My joy is in the pictures I take and share, joy in knowing He is the first and Last

I sit in silence, looking at the stars below the Heavens, seeing shooting stars ablaze
The winds of the spring blowing gently upon my face, my head is what I raise

I light the candle praying for you, I kneel looking to Our Mother and Her Son
In the Church He hangs upon the Cross, but He truly lives within, I no longer run

Playing in the snow, playing in the rain, skipping rocks, sitting by a camp fire
Holding hands, praising His name, roasting marshmallows, doing what He desires

Playing with cats with string, watching Liz laugh with Joy, seeing an inner peace
Listening to Dawn talk about her possum, this body we have is only a lease

Hearing the sounds of the night, the moon shinning, silence sitting with your father
Listening to country music with him, mom's eyes aglow, rising high upon the ladder

I find joy in the Grace to forgive myself, my Sins forgotten and wiped away
I find joy in long car rides looking at the country side, singing to the music I sway

I find joy in telling stories and in laughter, even more so when they come from you
I find joy in my work seeing hope in others eyes, listening to others points of view

I laugh and have fun in watching comedies, watching movies that make you think
I find joy when you give your opinion, in putting the pieces together and make a link

When I pray and read the Bible, feeling inner peace and strength I'm surrounded
Love burning deep within my soul, with Heavens guidance I know I'm grounded

Fun is listening to all your stories; Fun is your company no matter where I may be
Fun is watching you get excited over a donut; fun is in your love you give without fee

Fun is when we do tags on Thursday; fun is prank calling you when you're at the desk
Fun is you and I getting in trouble by Scott, fun is you, nothing more or nothing less

Fun is when you're distracted, when you play with your hair, and roll up my window
When I try to scream at the driver next to us, it's in knowing I will never let go

Fun is when we're getting ice cream and some woman wants a gallon of milk/cream
Fun is talking to you after work in the parking lot, listening to all of your dreams

So if you ever leave, please just know you'll always have a friend to remember
A friend that thinks the world and beyond of you, like an Angles voice as the Canter

So when you lay your head to sleep, my prayer will never cease forever you're at peace

For one day you be high above in Paradise, at the head of the table of our Lord's feast

I

September 26, 2017 (Revised)

I'm tired, exhausted, worn out, restless, weary, one last breath
I'm falling asleep at the wheel, I need an
escape, a release, and I'm cooped up

I need silence, I need time out to listen to
nature, and I need to get away
I'm bothersome, I'm cumbersome, I'm in the way, and I'm needy

My prayers seem useless, I'm idle, I'm weak,
I'm foolish, the laughingstock
The black sheep, the goat, filled with excuses,
I'm unfocused, sidetracked

My body aches, I'm a failure, I'm lazy, take
this pain from me, replace me
Good night I say, but there's a voice within
saying rise, fight the good fight

Feeling within your mind the alcohol permeates
into your veins, getting you high
Justifying whether or not this could be the
night, the demons weight heavy

I do this all myself with only God as a force,
his presence and glory is enough
I ignore the help of man, trust is not in my
vocabulary, the spark within grows

Though I feel there's nothing left inside, I don't
go off the cliff, I wait out the night
Every angle weighs in, I avoid the outside
noise and clutter, my head screams

I confess my failures and shortcomings; my
sins though heavy do not define me
My pride and my ego seem all distant now;
are there any hero's left to lean upon?

I will not fade into the night; no, not this
night; I will carry on till the morning
Though the day hasn't ended, I will drift off
and slip into its future, in abandon

My Lord will not leave me to the wolves, I
am guarded from up above on high
This world leaves me little to no hope, but my
God counts every hair upon my head

I sit here and wait, addiction has been my
close companion for years; my enemy
It sits there with me, offering a drink, to
inhale death, feed personal pleasures

But I will not fade into the night! Not tonight!
I will sit here, wait, and pray silently
Saints and Angels sing, bow down to the
righteous one, praying for me tonight

They do not cease, I am accounted for, though
hopeless as it seems, I'm guarded
I will stay put tonight, I will not give in this
day, hope is all I have, and it's enough

Eyes Are All Around Me

September 28, 2017

Eyes are all around me, watching my every move at hand
The voices speak in every language, Tower of Babel in the sand

Leaders of yesteryear stuck in hell, living their days without rest
Kingdoms of power beyond comprehension, for I can attest

I'm seeking the truths of the evil, its falsehood; its wicked lie
For I wade in the pits of Hades, the fowl stench without blue sky

Nimrod lives again, released from his prison, his reign never ended
Pressure is upon my days weighing, in the darkness of night I vented

Thoughts of starting once again embrace, my inner strength failing
Looking above I'm powerless, like having
no wind at all when sailing

I'm stagnant, I'm angry, yet I have hope, because of you I move on
Felling I'm stuck upon the sinking sands on the shores of Babylon

Their eternity of bliss is hell, while beauty
awaits me on the other side
He builds us castles beyond measure; from
this moment enjoy the ride

They'll be only one language, a language
of love, light filling my being
For the final horn blows in the night, the watching eye always seeing

I stand here with the armor of God, with
an army of angels at my side
Legions upon legions preparing for war, having no more tears to cry

I'm beyond the point of paranoia; I'm beyond the point of no return
I'm driven to the edge of the cliff looking down, feeling no concern

For I'm set in my stance, I know it is time, the constellations aligned
The powerful, the deceiver, the eye upon the pyramid is the sign

The markings of the beast are in plain sight, tattooed and cursed
My words on my lips are truthful indeed, now is the time to reverse

Go back to the beginning, where it was for the love of the moment
Instead of just a chore, falling victim to hate, now it's time to own it

Feeling ignorant to what's out there, knowledge escapes my grasp
Being lost in a desert, the thick of forest, it was never meant to last

I ride on all intuition, the inner voice within speaks to me softly
Sickness spreads and divides, choices are crucial and can be costly

Praying to heaven for my thoughts not to race, anxiety runs astray
My eyes shift to my Lord, keeping me humble, focused, array

The giants of yesteryear flex muscle, though demons rip their flesh
For upon entrance to the underworld all
strength is lost in the depths

One mustn't ever escape the deceiver's claws, his teeth clinch, grind
There those beg for the scraps of the table, though they once dinned

Feasted, drank and were merry, excess the only way they ever knew
For now the beauty, sex, and women are gone, we've been led askew

Searching for answers to questions unclear, he wishes to trade places
For he knows his time is short in number, filling in the empty spaces

He lays there in a state of coma not rest, fighting off the horror
The thoughts of the past return with furry,
fearing his own tomorrow

The riddles become more complex, yet
they scream out from the page
The wars you've forged inside your mind are set, done, you've waged

Bargained for more than you could afford, more than you can chew
For the time awaits us both, my friend,
what is your choice, me or you?

Stories, Myths, and Legends

September 30, 2017

Where did I come from? How did I arrive?
The earth hides these secrets not easily contrived

Stories, myths, legends; plenty to say and tell
When will I no longer burn, escape the pits of hell?

These bones decay, this flesh fades, my mind falters
Why must we kill ourselves, rape our own daughters?

What happened to selfless love, honesty, and giving?
Did we forget to honor thy parents, and be forgiving?

We desecrate the flag, the honor, and the lives lost
Along the way we forgot our hero's, and all the costs

The price they paid for their homage, sickened minds
Twisted bodies, fragmented, mental health never finds

Righteous and wrongdoing, lost along the way
To be in their suffering mind for a minute, just a day

The people at the top have laid the ground rules
Us pawns take the bait, kneel, disrespect like fools

Unity lost somewhere in our pride, we're ignorant
Waste pools filled with rot, water motionless, stagnant

God breathed us into life, what else was there before?
Angels, giants, beasts; these questions I cannot ignore

My mind is filled with doubt, answers I demand
Though nights are horrid, I'm dismantled, glass to sand

The day ends with silence, in it I pray for answers high
The new day begins with darkness; its secrets cannot hide

The ancients of old revealed, chapters within a book
Lessons written upon scrolls, we must give a second look

Galaxies in the billions, stars as countless as the sands
Peering into the past we gaze, crossing oceans to far lands

Offspring, forgotten generations, foreign to our knowledge
Wives, daughters, husbands, sons, commoners paying homage

Temples forgotten in time, pyramids forged in mountains
Gold as gods, money as power, life everlasting water fountains

Beams of light traveling in space, returning to their creation
Man waiting without realization, moon in orbit, space station

Am I the only one left? Though sinful ways are exploited
Is there another amongst us also? The truth cannot be avoided

Two paths soon will cross, forming a bond making a knew
This fact cannot be dissolved not broken, old and young feud

The ancients will retreat while the young will soon prevail
The gift is coming in form of man, secrets will soon be revealed

Amidst the Stars

October 3, 2017

I'm lost within the moment; the moment is gone for good
The future is the present, for the past is so misunderstood

The moon bleeds into the horizon, glowing burning bright
Tides are moved by its immense nature, its glorious sight

My nerves have reached a peak, a pinnacle amidst the stars
Obstacles obstruct the truest view, not having to look far

Vehicles fly timeless through space, traversing time itself
Peering into the eyes of God, a glimpse of God's wealth

For the moments we have are precious more than gold
For the physical nature only last so long within the fold

The disc burning bright within the sky settles and sets
Gone for now but not for long, too soon one sadly forgets

The past rears its ugly head, forgotten amongst written scroll
Burned evidence wasted knowledge; time has taken its toll

The night hides his truth, my solitude both friend and foe
For in the moments alone I ponder, in time I will surely know

The gates of the universe are infinite, beyond are imagination
Man's mind cannot fathom reality, and all of God's creation

The darkest of moment's right before the dawn, I seek truth
For eyes are cold in the world we live, age betrays the youth

A man stands amongst his own mind, making his own universe
A world of darkness set apart from reality, evilness dispersed

I feel the tension, it's in the air, and we're set against each other
Daily the tides rip me to pieces, once friends we are no longer

Upon the top of the world the warped sifts out others one by one
Changing scores upon scores of lives, cowardly he hides and runs

My heart is heavy in this moment, the tension takes my mind
We're robots programmed to hate, molded on an assembly line

For the past has come up to bit us, even the truth is bent, frayed
There is no ending good in sight, we're bought, sold and made

Set against each other, formed into groups, placed in neat piles
Numbers are tallied up in arrangement, and for the while

Libraries destroyed taken out of the equation, we're dismissing
Disregarding the awe of life, the noise consumes, not listening

The turmoil is within us, the fight is daily within the mind
I've fallen once again upon the rocks, my choices, my crimes

To whom shall we depend upon? Why shall they give us truth?
For their agendas are just that, they play us like pawns, led askew

How do we peer into one's soul, acknowledging our differences?
Yet pardoning our sins deeply, we're wounded in all instances

Soon the sky shall give light to day, yet darkness persists
Blackening out the daylight like an eclipse, sent into the abyss

I now am the darkness, at times the light, never in between, gray
Yet I've been brought to mountain peaks and beyond to stay

Seen the empires, revealed the truth, lowest among the ranks
Like a wave in sea traveling in faith, hitting the shores banks

I'm drowning daily, yet kept afloat, my God hasn't abandoned
For the prayers haven't ceased yet, though I'm in the cannon

The seas may rise, the mountains may crumble, and tides may shift
But yesterday, today, and tomorrow are his, I'm counted on his list

I Am

October 3, 2017

I am the sea, the water, lakes and streams
I am the life which represents love, removing the beam

The splinter in your eye I have removed, therefore I am
I am the breath of everlasting life, I am in which I am

The earth, the sky in which you see, I give it all to you
The stars, the very oxygen you breathe, every breath taking view

I am the wheat, the barley grain, the grape upon the vine
The bread upon your table and feast, words of love so fine

The wind at your back, the downhill trot, a place to rest your head
I am the earth in which you reap and sow, two bound and wed

The job when you needed it the most, almost down and out
Holding your head high, the confidence when you wanted to doubt

The hand holding you up until the race is done
The yoke bore for you, a face radiant as the sun

I am the salt of the earth, the seasoning in your meal
When your thirst is quenched in the desert,
I am the satisfaction you feel

Justice, bravery, peace, are just a few words to describe
I am the shining light that cannot be extinguished, and cannot hide

Powerful, mighty indeed, greatest amongst them all
Your prayer answered without void, the one who's taken the fall

I am the simplicity and awe of the moment, the call
Always walking at your side, giving second chance to Saul

Many of names have been given to me, Holy One, Spirit, Father
The heavens I have created for you, billions of exquisite color

Gifts given to make you smile, calmness amongst the sea
The wind to guide your course, somewhere you always can flee

I am the Son given as sacrifice, your hope, the reason
The beauty of the snow, color of fall, summer, spring, the seasons

The perfect plan, the purpose, the ultimate pinnacle, the summit
All-encompassing power of space and time, to you I commit

Never lay your head down low, never fear or regret
For I am the one that will never let go, this shall you not forget

Memories Consume

October 6, 2017

Waiting for a hand to help you off the ground
Waiting for a touch, gently whispering a sound

Sounds of the night where I feel you the most
Tender soft hands, you're humble, you never boast

I'm left here wondering, will I ever see you again?
They say time heals all wounds, I miss you my friend

When will I get my day, that day in the sun to shine?
Will I ever see your face again? I walk that fine line

Between where you are and where I am, I'm sinking
I have too much time on my hands, too much thinking

I have to sit back and reflect, memories consume
These walls are closing in; I'm all alone in this room

Voices start to speak to me, the drug hits my veins
Will the night ever end? It seems all it does here is rain

The walls are my prison cell, surrounding me on all sides
I miss the times we would run off together, go for a ride

Ride into the summer night, forgetting all of our problems
Safe and sound from our stresses, companionship solved them

Nothing last forever, but I'd give all to you in a heartbeat
For you was my love; now there's just an empty seat

A seat that will always be waiting for you with open arms
For love never dies, I sit here waiting trying to be calm

Calm because I'm numb, I cannot feel anymore, I'm not sane
Where will I run to, where can I find shelter from the rain?

Three thousand miles seems so very far and so distant
But if you'd just call I'd be there in a flash without resistance

I wonder what you're doing now, do you ever think of me?
Do you miss me as much as I miss you? I'm caged, not free

I put you on this pedestal; my image of you is so high
I see you in the distance, your soul raises, touching the sky

I fall off to sleep, images of you dance in my mind
I've never met someone quite like you, you're so kind

You'd give without question, never asking anything in return
For one last kiss to thee, haunting images sear and burn

Into my memory for eternity, time fails to separate this gash
Hell must be this everlasting feeling, teeth grind and gnash

Though knowing you at least gives me hope for tomorrow
For the moments I spent with you are mine, I didn't borrow

Borrow the time given, it is mine to keep, cherish all days
For walking with you hand and hand, I've counted all the ways

One day I'll see you in heaven, you'll be an angel with wings
You'll be amongst the stars up above, forever I will sing

Knowing you'll be safe for all time from the storms in life
Finally all pain will be washed away from me, all my strife

    The day begins and ends, hope is light for all to see
    Thank you, my friend, it will be forever you and me

Head Rest Wearily

October 6, 2017

Head rest wearily on a pillow made of steel ablaze
Wondering where rest will come, we're lost in the maze

Walking into walls pointing us nowhere, never getting out
Stuck in a bind, we blindly run like rats as we shout

The fire keeps us tame, in awe struck by its immensity
At bay we're kept, as the coals are added to keep intensity

Books have led one astray, information overload excites
Pure bliss and fantasy at the brink, like man's first flight

Into blue skies even further, to space, beyond imagination
Our heads and minds like ants marching, kept in conjunction

Sitting in our cubicles, waiting for the day to end and begin
Collecting our dirty money, we're lifeless, deadly as sin

Not knowing what is true, what are false? Backs against the wall
We're tired, drawn to waters of poison, ready for a certain fall

Learning from history can save us, the educated and elite know
Our world is burning to the ground; what do we reap and sow?

Knowledge is most powerful, the commoner is much divided
The poor are the wicked pawns, the weak are the undecided

The debt grows in furry, as interest is paid on top rampant
The situation rises to its climax, ignites like match to accelerant

We dig a hole, a ditch, burying ourselves in our own grave
The darkness of the night prevails, caught in the tidal wave

Dragged out to see by the undertow, the currents take us deeper
One of us shall rise from the depths; he will be called the seeker

The energy grows with every moment, the morning draws day
Early autumn dies beautifully turning color, like children we play

Soldier overseas knows not his sin, laughed upon and mocked
For the greed of man slaughters minds, mouths shut and locked

They throw away the key, tossing it into the pits of the abyss
All seems lost forever, though they're forgetting God's list

The code is in the text, the solution is in the mix, on the rise
For God's humor is in such ironies, sometimes God does lie

I found this truth out in my darkest moment, in a torturous state
Looking into cold blackened eyes, of the mindless whom rape

One day justice will prevail, to precedence, rise overall
Holding a chokehold over man, for he soon will answer the call

Humanity will respond in a most unusual way, stabbing knives
In darkest moments we become desperate, intermingling lives

Murderous indeed, sending the guilty to the dungeon and pit
Where incriminating remarks will supersede, irony and sure grit

For the pillow tonight gathers no heat or head to lay to rest
The crimes have been forgiven from above, no more no less

Man Behind the Wall

October 7–8, 2017

Walking through the autumn wood, colors of red, orange, yellow
Green forest awakens with life, winds pass through gracefully

Skipping rocks on the shore, motionless waters still, quiet thoughts
For a moment all worries forgotten, the man moves without notice

Ahead up in the distance, waiting, watching, peering from afar
The calls from the island, bird seeking
refuge, watching from the shore

Keeping pace as the pangolin swings,
steady in the race, voices raised
For the quiet and serenity of the forest is disturbed, just phases

Pictures left behind at the scene, images, moving frames in motion
The lakes separated, long road, summer scorching sun, burning skin

Thoughts of yesteryear come to mind,
drunken man, homeless, alone
The man is ragged, same height, lighter
build; green eyes in the night

Peering into the eyes of his father, blackened soulless, disconnected
The rage fills their thoughts, the emptiness between them grows

The forest once their friend now so far
away, sunsets forgotten, hollow
The pavement cold, once what was steel,
plastic, tearing falling apart

The two connected by fates twisted, mistakes
multiply, pointing fingers
The roads meet at the fork, the choice now must be made, options

Turn back, go forward; take the turn, all
roads lead to an abyss so deep
There's only one hope left, the thought comes and goes, screaming

The days grow short; the truth cannot be truth with a lie, or deceit
Accidents number up, they're on edge as the road comes to an end

The man is in the shadows of the wood, waiting in the dark, regrets
Baseball game forgotten, on the diamond
he stands alone, ship sinking

Lights go down, go out, she casts tears of
running water, shaking hands
He stares into lifeless eyes, beaten down, smells so pungent; rearview

The objects seem so very far, close to touch, yesterday won't go away
Night wind blows as the darkness moves on, glassy eyes, empty

No words, blank stare and look, mother screams aloud from within
The wood so familiar with the eyes of the
man, behind the wall he waits

Watching in the night, wondering nomad,
man of many names, faces
Their eyes are upon me, he waits in the
shadows behind the stonewall

I have been found out, so have you, mistakes
of plenty fill the hallways
Smashing dreams, she laughs aloud, feuding family torn apart

Children laughing, playing, man in his thoughts, narrowly escaping
The grave cannot hold back what it
contains, demons gather together

Blood trickles down his face, cold to touch, old man in the shadow
Child unaware, doubt, fear, anxiety fill the empty days ahead

He's coddled, never grew up, never on his own, unable to escape
The curse grows stronger with time; they
trade places, empty thoughts

Arrogance and ignorance fill his nights, filling in the emptiness
A boy was once filled with life, striving to excel, succeed, achieve

The poison intoxicates his mind, summer nights filled with sickness
The man waits in the shadows, watching,
observing; thief in the night

Autumn winds blow to wherever they
please, nights go on, unceasing
Last of the warm wind blowing, a child at his side, screaming within

The woman wakes in the night, changing history's course; waiting
He's never too far away, in the darkness slipping into the night afar

Driving the street where it all began,
moonlit sky, stars shinning bright
Boy morphs into old man behind the
counter, sleepless nights awake

The statue holds its ground, time starts
catching up with the mishaps
Remembering what has occurred over his
history, hands on the clock

Small town contains hidden knowledge, holding back many secrets
Driving, staying awake, music of yesterday
on the radio, window down

The past meets the future without hesitation,
the present lost in between
Sentenced to a life of soberness, old man
sits on his porch, anticipating

Light on in the kitchen, old house once filled
with life, through the window
One eye opened, keeping a close watch,
crashing into the wall of fate

Moon stretched across the midnight sky,
clouds low rushing for cover
Winds howl, unseasonably warm, elongated summer, never ending

Paths intertwined, autumn takes its final stand, children laugh; play
Giving themselves to the darkness for
pleasures of the world, sickness

Room small, smells of hospital fills his senses, what did he do wrong
Boy trapped in his mind, his body, his soul scarred and wounded

Life not meant for him to understand, not
his own, leaves change color
The stonewall waits, fading over time,
weathered, old man behind the wall

Alongside the Lamb

October 10, 2017

Heartbeat, rhythmic sounds, all in the palm of his hand
All fear, doubt, and misery gone, no longer no, but I can

Gentle waves tossed amongst the shore, tranquil thoughts
For a moment all is lost but not forgotten, the truth sought

The lion sleeps alongside the lamb, viper with the child
Poisonous is the snake bit, as it's been there all the while

Though miles separate the family, love can and will attest
For it speaks in volumes above all else, filters out the rest

She's born to the world, quiet night, still cloud and moon
Something doesn't seem right in place, I'm gone too soon

The light cannot be contained, a spark ignites in space
Deepest depths never reached or touched infinitely laced

Encompassing, embracing the unknown, for we know not
Our minds and capability finite; our pride, our lust, our rot

The awesomeness of the break of day, words cannot describe
Night filled with sounds of summer, love cannot easily hide

Here there isn't judgment; there isn't shame, though remorse
Forgiveness, tolerance are what matters, love is the source

It supply's, giving without asking in return, selfless indeed
The signs which bring forth love are extravagant and lead

Stableness and certainty come with faith in God and God alone
For without his love we have nothing, into the desert we roam

Generosity is his nature, his character above all things
The unity and bond of man couldn't compare, angels sing

We've strayed away from his ways, wondering with thirst
No water could quench anyone, for without him we're cursed

The storms of life break the levy, in his presence we succeed
5,000 men given bread, fish multiplied; promise he would feed

Miracles were preformed, parables were told to the masses
Turn a blind eye in ignorance; we were cracks in the glasses

The day is given by light; the darkness covers the lies in place
The rejected one is now the cornerstone, I can see his face

My persistence, my drive, my inner most fear and pain erased
These few things separated by design are caught up into space

Distances seeming most near and far between lasts forever
Though his forgiveness never ends, my sin I must endeavor

Obedience is a virtue; we must continue to work on improving
Prayer is my guide and strength, his words are most soothing

Stones left in the stream are smoothed out, formed over time
Molded and shaped into his image gracefully, given a sign

A reminder of our jaggedness, how he buffs out our rust
Making us whole, new; time is on our side though we're dust

The chosen aren't bound by the enemy, we our God's children
Sounds of the stream are one, as far as east from west our sin

The time has come; the celebration is at hand at our fingertips
For what pleases he is grace, the words of love upon our lips

Therefore our obedience is his gift; I will not tremble or fear
It's no longer no but yes I can; he is always by my side near

Vengeance Certain Rage

October 11, 2017

Crash-landing into the netherworld, escaping your own self
Nothing, no money in the world could buy or accumulated wealth

Like a robot to the computer, responding to all demands
Salivating a bit, for a bone, a reward for the master's command

Working tirelessly, endlessly into the night and darkened morn
Seeming to never cease for rest, wishing for the king, the norm

What is normal anyway, does it have a face or image to draw?
Does it where a crown or does it get mocked, having any flaw?

Leading the witness to believe, giving one false hope, illusion
Being amongst all that is unreal, being the source of confusion

The day comes with vengeance, the night ends with certain rage
Being locked up for years in a prison cell, released from my cage

I'm here he now says, tell all of my coming, answer to only me
For I am death, I am glory, where will one go, where will one flee?

Time has stopped, you have been figured out, there is no way out
For I see you at all times, you can run and hide, scream and shout

Though you cannot hide for long, every corner I will search
In the shadows and darkness, I take refuge, I creep and I lurch

Leaving all in torment, for mine has swiftly approached, has come
There's little left to have all is taken, all there is now is to run

Arrogance, head held high, spitting upon God's chosen few
Disregarding one's silent accomplishments, grotesque and lewd

Out of place is the feeling, from the moment I arrive and leave
Comfort has been left in the past, only lies now do I weave

Spider webs woven, extrinsically, elegantly, skillfully made
Born from the darkness, trapping one within slowly they fade

Paralyzing, numbing the body and soul, feeding them fables
Coaxing one into deception, unsteady hand less than stable

Cornered like a rat, trapped with bait, a hook, loosed to the dogs
Evil spirits released amongst mankind, fallen angels in the fog

From afar look like gems, they're here to tear apart our souls
Here to answer to nothing but themselves, and take control

Swaying their bodies, swinging their hips, peering in our eyes
Dancing silhouettes riding in the night, sucking man dry

I've seen them in the streets, businesses, you cannot escape
All one has now is regret, left with bitterness, always irate

Old, young, everything in between are in on the masquerade
We will certain vanish without a trace, into the darkness fade

He has been let loosed for a season; his time is near, at hand
Our crimes have caught up with us, we're castles made of sand

The drug has hit the streets; the gangs are out in full force
The alcohol permeates, the sail, bow of the ship run their course

All I feel is like giving up, laying down my defenses, my head
Giving into the hatred, the bile, the lies, and all which is dead

The demons gather round, screaming in the night and beyond
Looking in my eyes I'm found out, what is right and wrong?

We are pawns and puppets, control has been forgotten, lost
The cockpit is ready for takeoff; we're now counting all costs

You'll find us here waiting, you cannot fathom the immensity
The significance of this night is important, hoping for simplicity

The day breaks, near future brings forth what you may doubt
For in the silence is the answer you're looking, what it's all about

The sun beckons the call, the plan, the early morning gives way
6,000 years has taken place for this moment, for this very day

As I is written from both dawn till dusk, beginning to end
Every chapter leads to another, and now the climax begins

Beautiful Mishaps

October 13, 2017

Facing the crowd, eyes stare upon your inner most thoughts
Moments not to be forgotten, memorable, frozen in fear

Mind never staying in the moment, speak without contemplation
Out of turn, interruption, fleeing from your inner self, questioning

The voice at the controls, pushing the button, pulling the lever
At the wheel one falls asleep, falling fast, disassembling

He makes amends with his creator, yet the crowds stare upon
They watch without ever noticing, searching for the truth

Vicious cycles repeated methodically over time, head pounding
Waiting to reach the edge of the world, falling off into the abyss

A kiss starts a new beginning, paralyzing, forcing a hand
Tender sweet the moment, recollections of the past rear its head

Hunger fills the belly, music out of tune, voices tell the story
Nothing held back, beautiful mishaps, mistakes forgiven

Conversation ending abruptly, never satisfied, life of denial
The car is warm, cool autumn night, the stars shine; go unnoticed

His hands are dirty, the process repeated, the cuts run deep
Excuses fill the mind, the disease takes the evening once again

Wanting to act upon, holding back, the dark force creeps slowly
Whispering, speaking in the ear not to make a move, repent

Start again, from where it all began, a fresh new sheet of paper
The day lives in infamy, eternal everlasting life, he calls me

Illusions aren't real; the damage cannot be reversed, heavy heart
The struggle is in the moment, a peace overcomes him, serene

Words of wisdom revealed before him, there's more to this
Meeting by accident would be irresponsible to ponder upon

Who is this woman, why has she been sent, what is the meaning?
The questions cut like knives, forcing his hand, his reality

Vanity, self-centeredness, falsehoods, the deception of beauty
How does one get to this moment? The road has been long

Quirkiness is his nature; beauty escapes his outer core and shell
Trying to make impressions everlasting, attacking man's faults

Self-inflecting wounds, rubbing salt into them, unbearable
Woman are stronger, rage fills man's mind, jealousy his heart

Bearing the burdens of the world, their sin, paying the debt
The punishment fits the crime, knowledge is what one seeks

Peace in the moment, rage in the seconds, minutes at hand
Making the pilgrimage, miles seem so long, second thoughts

Seasons change, sunburned skin, weathered, unrecognizable
The young naïve, arrogant, prideful, careless their actions

The stage is set, the leader charismatic, the audience in awe
The new day rises, he comes like a cloud, fog upon the waters

Facing the crowd, he now is a new man, steady his ways
Confidence encompasses his being; all eyes are upon him now

Water, Bread, and Wine

October 2, 2017

Steps taken in faith, wounded by the past, life's regrets
Forgiveness by penance, sitting upon ash, all he forgets

For our mistakes and misshapes are all wiped away
Making us whole and pure without blemish, not frayed

Like a child walking by faith alone, patience, just being
Walking amongst wolves, protected by the son, the spirit

All falls around him, crashing walls, plummeting down
I hold my head held high, knowing not the world around me

Circumstances given I should feel beaten, yet I'm renewed
Renewed, recharged by the coming of the new day, replenished

Blindly I walk into the night, he lights my world ahead
For I sleep in his arms and rest well, by faith alone I'm fed

No water or bread can sustain my health, only the Holy Ghost
For his gift of grace freely given, only in the Lord shall I boast

Questions led to more questions, our knowledge is faulty
The more one thinks they know, ignorance bliss but is costly

Though I walk through the valley alone, thirsting for truth
Hungry for bread, nourishment one doesn't live upon alone

He gives the bread of life, the bread his body, wine the blood
We walk wounded, he is the crutch, the caregiver, the amen

The stars obey his command, he is the word, he is the constant
Running, never growing weary, the holy one which was sent

I'm still, waiting for his beckon, my burden upon his shoulders
My purpose is his purpose, living for him alone he's in control

Though I feel stagnant and paralyzed, seeming never to move
I am in constant motion, trusting him, his timing impeccable

Living free isn't enough for me; though I'm a slave I'm his
For freedom is knowing the other side awaits, therefore I'm free

I sit upon the ash, knowing we will suffer what's to come
Repentance is all we have left, into his arms I shall run

Forever Linked

October 16, 2017

Compromising your feelings, your morals, going to great length
Casting away all you've accomplished, your mind, all your strength

Dying a thousand deaths couldn't compare, eyes empty, hollow
Wishing upon a wishing well is useless, the mindless will follow

One by one they vanish, disappear into nothing, wasted and worn
Giving up for the taking, violent waves high, storms of life rage on

A peaceful moment money can't buy, comes light upon his soul
The pages worn with time empty and blank, the story unfolds

Happiness is achieved by understanding, relationships evolve
Changing for the better of one's sanity, not all problems are solved

One man's treasure is another's waste, thrown to the fire to be burned
Morphed into incense risen to the four winds prevailing which churn

Timeless pieces, things seen and heard priceless, cherished moments
Sitting round table breaking bread, children laughing, restful

Their eyes wondrous filled with excitement, forgetting all trouble
For here worries are cast aside, tossed, separated left from right

Predetermined and planned is mere illusion, fate results in decision
Decisions thought about by the designer, fear comes from superstition

Ghosts from the past creep up, what was swept under the carpet
Accumulates over time slowly, manifestation builds, divide, conquers

Never get lost in another, you'll be let down hard in the end, drowning
The journey brings lots of ups and downs, the thought is astounding

We've come to a crossroad; a pretty face could be certain death
What looks shinny and precious could be fatal, regret is all that's left

How does one fall in love without distraction, someone's male intent?
I'm tired of the lies and deceit, testimony to the truth is why I was sent

Resentment of poor decisions, mistakes, the how and why's sink in
Questions and doubts wrap their arms tightly, death comes to our kin

Our relationship with extremes could be deadly, opposites attract
Negative and positive charges give way, upon this moment I react

Alone now stress is dissipated, the blood freely courses through vein
Bringing new life breaking down barriers, we're different not the same

Showers come down watering the world below, filtering out waste
The haze from the filth of man vanishes, the coming day sighs

Taking a deep breath is vital, immortality comes from hope and trust
The sound of the trumpet blazes loud and clear, worry from the enemy

Eyes are the windows to the soul, the face staring back causes vanity
Ugliness rears its head like one's wicked past, like tragedy, calamity

The choices one makes brings forth at times fruit, weed, or thorn
Therefore one must remember to choice wisely, makers' hands form

Either beauty or disgust is shaped from the sculptor, clay hardens
Though once formless coming forth from the earth, breathed into life

The man falls into deep sleep, the rib gives way to the woman
Flesh made from flesh, the two bound by each other, forever linked

The ramifications could choose to be most dreadful, you must decide
Is this worth fighting for? The next chapter awaits, it is what's inside

Road Coming to a Fork

October 14, 2017

Windows to the soul, blue glaze, wisdom beyond measure
Let go, it's not all that important, let be what is to be

You're too hard on yourself; you've come so far, my friend
Just relax, it's going to be fine, I've been here all along

Meeting someone you've felt you've known for years
Goodnight, my friend, take care, all is well, it's never too late

In relevance to the grand scheme of things it's miniscule
I'm running out of time it feels like, righteousness at hand

Woman at the well fetching water for a king, bended knee
You look familiar, you're humble, and I'm relaxed at bay

Trickling rain falls upon the fields, replenishing the crops
It trickles upon your face, turning gloomy days calm, at ease

The light peers through the window, you're astonishing
You're astounding, amazing, gracefully you carry yourself

The chanting is therapeutic, rhythmic, sweet sound of angels
Running in golden fields on a spring day, warmth on shoulders

Walking the trail that leads home, warmth of the fire
Let it go, though the burden is most heavy, your time is at hand

The road has come to the fork, let yourself be guided
The invisible hand of God, kind, understanding, gentle eyes

Slow to anger, rich in kindness, loving abundantly, forgiving
Heaven's warriors pray for me, saint's please intercede

For the time is upon us, the moment has arrived, be prepared
Putting on the armor of God, I'm am nothing without you

Kind eyes, blue skies, cross in the distance formed in cloud
Hand reaching out to me from the heavens, guiding me home

Crossing the finish line, hands held high, safe and sound
Almost there, my destination awaits me, the break of dawn

Lakeville

October 16, 2017

The lakes are a comfort when I'm sorrowful and down
They're inspiration for my soul, full of extraordinary sound

The lakes reflect my feelings, painted color reflects from above
The sky meets them on the horizon, intertwining with love

They're full of life in abundance, full of tranquility and bliss
The lakes offer opportunities so numerous, they're nature's kiss

They're my home away from home, they give me purpose
When the sun sets upon them, they're reflection that's reversed

The lakes gentle ripples arrive upon the shore, tender wave
Sometimes still like a picture frame, sanity miraculously saved

All paths and trails lead to the lakes, the views are immaculate
Though I left the lake once briefly, I'll always come back to it

The lakes are my anchor, my stability, my compass when lost
They guide me to safety; wash me clean, I'll pay whatever the cost

They collect the waters given from heaven, breath taking sights
I'll go to great lengths to visit them morning, afternoon, and night

The lakes have been my hope and happiness in times of distress
In times of despair they've given me encouragement, nothing less

So if you need motivation or just need a friend, the lake will be there
You'll never have to be alone, friend, you'll never have to despair

World Left Behind

October 24, 2017

The chains are broken, diamond cut divided
amongst the hungry, poor
The heavy load once bared by the lowliest, now the yoke is lifted

The bitter taste left in the mouths of the
just, suffering we must endure
For the vices of this life are deadly, such as these things we call cures

Upon the waste of stagnant waters, to still to drink from the pools
Poisoned are their contents to sustain life flowing, blackened death

The dead leaves collect making natural beds upon the green grass
Once summer held the fertile ground
below, now the fall brings turning

Turning of color within the background
of the forest and the canopy
The trees grow bare with every breath of wind blowing breeze

The birds scattered from east to west,
singing heard from miles on end
Man in a panic state runs impatiently,
wondering into the desert to die

Now I sit here and wait for my time to
arrive, waiting for no end in site
Cascade of brilliance lit across the horizon
meeting the sky embracing

Continuing to an eternity not yet fully
comprehended, unrecognizable
Glorious in abundance of celestial
magnificence, beauty, indescribable

Entering your mouth taste like honey, bitter
upon entering your stomach
The days of sun embracing your shoulders come to pass, rainy days

Winds howl from the north, embarking
on a new adventure, bitter cold
Come forth the early winters snow capping
the mountain range peaks

The day starts like any other, busy street
corners, haze of the headlights
Soon the traffic will give way to serine views of color, paths crossed

Moving mountains by his glorious hands
crafted by no other, mystifying
Without such a creator we are certain waste, meaningless lives

The warmth of the last true sun keeps me
afloat, westward I make my stand
The final approach awaits me at the pacific,
waves crashing all around

The coast calls forth my being; this is where I have been called to
From the out skirts of a foreign land in
disarray, scattered are the ashes

Circles form all around me, from our world
we live to outer space, vastness
Galaxies that will never be explored, our arrogance tells us otherwise

God alone knows these lands, their
uninhabitable conditions lay barren
A glimpse into the future, riding a light
beam for a thousand years or more

Coming back, fast-forwarding the future,
knowing not the world left behind
Like a fairytale, science fiction novel, never will the answers collect

Gather, manifest into the real world, for
whatever that means, my friend
For the business of our everyday lives hinder
our knowing and our reality

We our salt intertwined with the ocean
waters giving life to its inhabitants
Our voices though silent are heard from
our creator hands held in prayer

Crying out to the one above, giving recognition pleading for mercy
For the deceiver has planned a counterattack,
as he plans to set fire to all

Though in his rage the inferno made of
hot coals spills over, fire ablaze
The four corners of the world awaken
though in fear, moving slow, steady

Dismayed and disarranged are his thoughts, his memory altered
Messages from the silence of the night,
deep sleep overcoming the fear

The forces take charge as the black hole takes hold, drawing him in
Strangling the life from inside, choking out
all that is left within his being

Let loose from the underworld, a man without
a face lurks behind the curtain
Ready to strike with his army of soldiers forged from the fires of hell

Stench of decaying flesh, mixed with the
rotting waste thorn where he resides
His throne made of the bones of man, souls
lost forever, captured by mutiny

Hours marked by time calculated by earth's
measurement in accordance
Accordance to the rotation of spheres in
the heavens above, never lying

Fixed times and spaces, changes only in our mortal bodies trapped
Engulfed in skin we cannot escape until
the final resurrection foretold

The promises from the one before, while,
and beyond our comprehension
Past, present, and future known only by his knowledge above all else

The ending of the story has been written,
though our freewill is in play
For his wisdom is advanced, he is in control
of all, Lord over the righteous

Nothing is out of his reach, from the formation
of the universe and beyond
The heavens, the stars, the earth, and his greatest creation; man

The angels of heaven given to us as adversaries,
guides into uncharted realms
Reenergized and recharged as I live in this land, moving not an inch

My steps in comparison to the grand scheme of things is miniscule
Seeming yet insignificant to my creator and all he's accomplished

The relevance is all for nothing, yet he
loves me as if I was the only one
Each one of us his perfect creation made
complete through The Cross

Stardust are what make up our capsules,
worms shall we turn to in the ground
Dust making up are bodies before the end
time calling, tossed to the waves

Seafaring people, farmers, architects, all forms
of trade, called to set forth bread
Bread upon the table set to feast upon by
old, poor, young, everyone and all

The Outcast

October 24, 2017

She speaks amongst her friends in a casual manner and tone
She'll meet him later, the evening bleeding into morn

The frame stands still, as the pictures change from year to year
Witnessing timeless events, uncovering moments painted in time

Captured, frozen, dimensions, multi universes coming together
Though time stands still, the picture and frame deteriorate

Wood petrifies, steel to rust, fires melt away the past, the future
The night escapes his mind momentarily, distraction so beautiful

The ring is lost, forgotten; the gold is given up for ransom
The bond is betrayed by power and ultimate control, disassemble

The road leads him back to where it all started, the table
The morning of the slaughter, losing all hope in man, massacre

The sun comes up from the east over mountaintops
The shadows cast by the sun, early morning light shines forth

The man leaves his girl, his children at home, walking, hung-over
A small bond is formed, a kind act changing history's course

Our Lady, Our Mother, brings him many miles to a small town
New leaves are turned, the nightmare began; he's swallowed up

Eyes have not seen what I have seen; the ignorant laugh, mock
Their souls lost, the drunken minds cancerous, ignorance

We watch truths unfold in fictional story, characters, and lied to
I've looked into the eyes of the mentally insane, the outcast

I've met the forgotten, the hungry, the addicted, and the afflicted
I am the sword, the knife that cuts deep, the culprit

I thought I'd never walk again, staggering in the night, 3am
Counting the clock, the hands have stopped, the seconds seized

I hear you, you speak ill of me blatantly in front of me
While in mid conversation you slit my throat, you're a fraud

Stealing like a thief in the night the ones I love, care for
The plan has been set since the inception, the beginning

The fire rages without organization, without apathy, sympathy
The devil has many faces, speaks many tongues, worships himself

Jealousy, lust, hatred, revenge, words spoken to impress
In a slumber the war is waged, the pieces on the board assembled

Put them in a room and the worst of man shall be released
Unleashed from the bowels of hell, holding nothing back, last stand

We practice the same witchcraft as our ancestors, our enemies
Our philosophies, our religions, our political parties, the same

There aren't any new ideas, games of yesteryear are of yesteryear
Unoriginality is our candy, it has been done before, open your eyes

3 weeks of suffering, summer days and nights never gotten back
Sleepwalking, tearing into medal cabinets, painting the sky

Singing in a small room aloud, holding hands, she looks familiar
They speak to me as if they know me, they are angels in disguise

Games played, group secessions, it all falls into memory faint
I'm sorrowful, I'm defeated, too many sins to count, I'm lost

My habits catch up with me; I'm addicted and filthy, I'm wasted
My escape is the silence; my escape is the sounds of nature, peaceful

Day in and out I look for an outlet, a new start, a new beginning
I have nothing left to give, I'm empty inside, the weight is heavy

Reenergized, my eyes have rested upon the cloud set before me
Great is his reign, great is his kingdom high above, yet I fall

The journey has been so long; I'm afflicted, the wound is deep
The cut seems fatal, walk in a slumber down a long corridor

They speak to me saying go back to bed, you're sleep walking
The demons speak to me, I fall, I'm
drugged; they walk in the hallway

The sirens sound, they walk in the hallway in lines, chanting
I'm found out, sent to bed they come asking where I am, the one

I'm am hungry and tired, I read her favorite book, silently screaming
We gather round, he looks at me, I've been found out, and he runs

You know who you are, just remember are her words drifting away
Spoken softly, yet I recall in the silence,
the pictures on the wall stare

5 swans on the pond, 2 taken in the picture at the sunset, reservoir
Images are scrambled within my mind, games lost in translation

Angels call out my name surround me, I'm suffering, and I'm weak
She has covered great distances all around;
he is dazed from the drugs

Unimaginable are my everyday thoughts, confused, watchful eyes
Visits ending abruptly by paranoia, mother
and father left on the edge

Police sirens waiting in the distance, the splitting of lakes between
Shambles, all seems lost and forgotten,
stuck with cancer in my head

Where to go from here is a puzzle, a maze, will I make it out alive?
Sickened with the questions to this life and beyond, I'm frozen

Inquiring what do next, I look above and beyond to another world
Far and in between there lays the hidden
truths, impossible to reverse

Darkness and Light

October 18, 2017

Resistance is useless, the chapter that follows has been written
The enemy and his minions lurk, waiting for their opportunity

They react out of fear; fear of the unknown and uncertainty
What one doesn't understand is a direct threat to our existence

We shy away from the realties, covering ourselves from the light
Blinded are our eyes, the truth prevails, conquering out the night

They come full throttle, with full force, without any conscience
They hold nothing back; still their fear holds a tight grip, afraid

The thoughts of man are shattered by fallen angels
Beings sent from above to destroy the earth's inhabitants

Man! Man is on the verge of being eliminated from existence
An existence brought forth by the creator alone, separated

Separated by the destructive nature of the evil one
Lucifer once the great light, now darkened by the shadow

The darkness where he lays, cold, bitter, spreading disease
Why do we move on with so much hate, resentment?

Our chemical makeup is altered, shattered, manipulated
Our love is forever forgotten, wiped away by our ignorance

I stand upon the mountain, hands held high, there he is
He's amongst the clouds, calling out my name, glorious

The few will not slip into the shadows where the dead reside
   Where death holds certain precedence over the light

The light shall not be extinguished, the flame burns brightly
   The fallen angels fall back in rank, their strength is weakened

For our creator sends forth all of heaven, the great battle begins
   The ancients foretold of this; the gods would come from high

Descending upon me like a dove, like him that came before me
   We will attack; we will fight like brave men, and soldiers

My fear shall be wiped away, my God shall not leave, abandon
   I will prosper, we will excel and succeed; no evil shall prevail

The foul stench of hell fills my nostrils, suffocating on smoke
   Death fills the lungs of the fallen, fills their veins and blood

Blood saturated with the chemicals made, distributed by him
   The false one, the farce; comes full force with blade sharpened

Razor sharp are his fangs, poison within his arrows, stretching
   Sounds pierce like knives and penetrate into the flesh of man

Killing and wiping away the multiples, too many to count
   Accumulation multiplied by the millions, like flies they fall

Yet the light shall not be extinguished, he reigns on high above
   On the right hand side of the Father above waiting patiently

The minute, the day, the hour approaches; time stops suddenly
   The dragon comes forth falling from the stars above heavy

The fire falls from the skies, burning, torching the landscape
   The blood from men fills the rivers, flooding its banks, poisoning

The deceiver stands upon the peak looking down at his prey
The day comes forth; the dawn slowly approaches, methodically

The ancients were fully aware of the coming day, they're here
Amongst man, ready to do battle, paying homage to their creator

The magi foresaw the kings coming; coming from a holy family
The alignment has taken place, the stars burn bright, images

Images seen by astrologers, stargazers, prophets of old, beyond
As the stars we see now have dead long before, new ones ablaze

Their light shines forth in the depths of space, light years apart
The prophesies soon will come true, wailing, gnashing of teeth

First comes the rising of the enemy; then comes the chosen one
Elegant are his words, his speech, books written as knowledge

Knowledge from the tree in the garden, woman and man failed
A woman and man shall rise together, fighting fire and flame

The book is revealed to the world, the book of old, a beginning
A new start, a document with a blueprint, the alpha and omega

By the Boot Strings

October 24–25, 2017

The seas are raging, one more time, the last hurrah
The season holds a tight grip, patiently I await the change

The music plays to the beat of its own drum, soft, steady
The evening tells a story of its own, morning presses on

When will the telling day come? The time draws near
Time interchangeable, never out of sync, heavy storm

She watches me from afar, I can feel her presence
She waits for me to call, her bitterness and scorn forefront

Vengeance is upon her mind, she's confused, angry
She wants to come near, she finds any excuse

She's been held hostage all her life, she's in shadow
The night's moon is darkened by the clouded sky

The stars gone for now, the breeze rustles the trees
The dead leaves fall upon the grass, scared to move

Walking upon the grass barefoot, she's in silence
Quietly making her way towards the car, screaming

It's 3am, there's got to be a better way, we're alone
The hour has arrived, I'm forgiven; he's my refuge

Her car is warm; she gets in not knowing what's next
The ride is long, will the night ever end? Eternity

The joy within yourself is your strength, your passion, glory
Sleeping giants awaken within; stories of old give way

A shadow fills my soul as the day wears on, the young perish
Fade away, dust blowing in the desert, my eyes burning red

I'm losing faith in the youth; they respect nothing, no one
Their cutting words, cut throat behavior is disturbing

We are fading into the shadow of the night, the fog sets in
My hands are cracked, age is getting the best of me, I falter

Stained our hearts, are minds corrupt, poisoned, programmed
I am hot, I am cold, I am nothing in between, black and white

The pressures of the night pursue, lead me by the boot strings
The game changes, the playing field is transformed, manipulated

They wait upon my return, fake, forced smiles, tangents formed
Nothing seems to flow, bits and pieces come together

Nature calls out to me, grasping all there is left, crying
The young interpret the story to their own liking, hearts ache

He understands not his twisted mind, procrastination, back burner
Hoping things will go away, take care of themselves, confusion

I cannot save myself, I'm here now alone, I create animosity
Friction wears between the world I create, both real and fiction

The gun is now pointed at me, the shot is clear, the trigger set
Intervention is key to the victory, the storm gathers the waters

I am part of the youth by my childish
behavior, immature, arrogance
The night hides the truth of my shortcomings, my failures

The grays of this world are our excuses, great and small
Everything in between is explained away by our human nature

Now she stands in the night alone, storms rage on, inside and out
Man versus the boy, woman facing the girl inside; faceless

This time there is no meaning; there is no rhyme, graceless
We hold on to this imaginary world, lost and forgotten

Dismantling the Youth

November 2, 2017

It begins tonight, the rage set aside fading away
The stage is set for all to see, broken nation frayed

The young programmed to ignore, dismissing the truth
A nation once rich with values, now dismantling the youth

Left to the dogs our values, ripped to sheds livelihoods
Taken for granted the powers at be, losing our democracy

The right to choose, freedom traded in for false securities
Generations turn to a farce; lies are embraced by the ignorant

Turning a blind eye, in shadow they lick their chops, salivating
Standing in a corner naked for all to see, revealed, exposed

Walking down streets possessed by fallen spirits, homeless
Vengeance your only friend, incapacitated and enslaved

Your thoughts measured by the ruthless, the proud, arrogant
Flesh eating mongrels, selling their souls for seats of rot

The armies form from all nations, the enemy within borders
The names both foreign and domestic alike, meaningless

We wear the same uniform, pins made from plastic
Cheapened both the values of man and the trophies awarded

The rain falls on both the just and unjust alike, sun fading
From birth told to accept the rule at hand, pledging allegiance

An alliance to a rising power cancerous to all, an illusion
The enemy is within us, faceless without color or dialect

The unrelenting effort to disengage the righteousness
Separating us, sectioning us off as sheep brought to slaughter

A sacrifice in their eyes meaningless, we're numbers
The gate though narrow seems unobtainable, we're trampled

Tossed around in an endless raging sea amongst the storm
Divide and conquer the plan and goal; black, white, in between

Power transferred away from the people to kings and queen
Dictators, communism, socialism, they make our decisions

Code

November 5, 2017

Momentarily I feel bliss, it stays then it's gone
The moments last a second, my unfortunate song

Seconds turn to weeks, minutes turn to days
Days turn into months then years, wishing you'd stay

I found the note, the letter that you wrote to me
It brought forth a tear in my eyes, it wasn't meant to be

The pages stick together, time passes on eerily slow
I never did move on it's sad to say, now I wish to go

Waiting for your beckon, your call, patiently I wait
Thousands of miles we're apart tonight, it is now late

To be in shambles is ashamed, I'm falling behind
I seem to be in the shadows, star in the night the sign

It shoots through the universe, arriving most soon
Shinning for all to see, from the clouds descending moon

He rides on a white horse; he's in this very room
Cast aside as waste amongst man he now consumes

Called to do the duty of his father, call out kings, queens
Sorcery will be demolished, for his truth shall be seen

The ends of the earth have waited the moment and time
The farce preacher and prophet, no reason or rhythm

Your notes I have burned, both yours and hers too
All I have left is all but one, most important I have you

The driveway where we consummated our love, in your eyes
This is where I found true meaning; this is why I now cry

The key is in the notes you've obtained, paper and ink
You've known it to be true from the start, you mustn't blink

Soon there will be hailstone, hellfire to pay, cost is high
The arrival of polar opposites inevitable, angels now sigh

Come down from your slumber, you're intelligent, sacred
You've been chosen to witness, though you've been sedated

The storyline may be mixed, though the truth may be told
It lies between the lines that are clear; it's marked by the fold

So this I say to you, the day now soon approaches, it's near
There's nothing left to say, my friend, hold this true and dear

When the world comes crashing down, keep your head high
The end is just the beginning; these are truths, not lies

The Comet

November 11, 2017

The dragon comes to conquer the tales that once were foretold
The streaks of blue, green, light the winter's sky above cold

My thoughts are blurred, placing pointing fingers, laying blame
The past so close but out of reach, yet somehow I feel the same

I stared upon the still waters, moon shinning bright on high
Looking for the answers to questions, time I cannot buy

The treetops looked so different that night, swaying in the breeze
I shivered once or twice clasping hands, the cool air I breathed

The beginning to the year that fateful night, changing me forever
Leading me down paths of ups and downs, challenges to endeavor

Solitude I looked for in the night, a peaceful place to rest
The sandy shores I stood upon, nothing more, nothing less

The wooden log I sat upon, wishing upon the night at hand
The stars twinkled in the heavens, my spirit high above the land

The stillness of the evening, no person by my side to hold
Feeling as if she's gone forever, never again to be in the fold

Yet that light across the sky was awesome, like touching her face
Kissing her goodnight, smelling her skin, memories do not erase

A war I wish to fight, to get back what I had once lost
A sword I will bring up to strike, no matter what the price or cost

Eras go by, time doesn't cease, and my love never dies or falters
Though mistakes have cost me much, I make enemies my brothers

I'm the peace maker, I'm the voice of reason, and I'm here to say
Though time separates generations, all mankind will not go astray

I recall the smell in the air that night, chimneys glowing ambers
The pine scent filled the brisk air, beautiful like the churches cantor

Her voice like an angel sent from above, every note flawless
The night a child was born to redeem the world, my eyes teary mist

The meek will inherit the earth a wise man did once say
For the truth I have come to tell to all, so excuse me if I may

Tell you the coming of a prophet, one before me, never he sleeps
For he knows what's coming next, deep secrets he does keep

The east is where the flame burst from the sky, green and blue
The split between the ponds is where it's found, beach side view

Letters offered up to the heavens, burned as incense aflame
Though these vivid memories last a lifetime, one letter remains

Won't you start my fire, won't you hand me the torch?
Of course I've known it from the very start, this I will not abort

They're told from the start to disregard what they cannot see
If you cannot touch, hold, or see it, it's a fable to both you and me

Receding shores, droughts and rainless days, nights came to pass
This sickness that crept in my life is illusion and will not last

The winds came crashing upon the shore, tossing to and fro
The camera took the photographs, and soon all will see and know

Preparation

November 14, 2017

Preparing for a perfect storm through imperfect eyes and hands
The planets cross paths once again like
two grains on the seashore sands

Heavens blotted out with a covering blanket silver gray, unseen
Blind trust is all I have now, some call it
faith, I call it plain out believing

I've seen the devil; preparation is the key,
his final push I cannot foresee
For his unrelenting rage sometimes unpredictable,
into the desert I must flee

In less than a day, less than 24 hours I will
meet the next step in my life
What shall I say, what's the next step?
Despite all of my energy and strife

I don't know whom to trust, where to turn,
where to lay my head at night
For all I have is the one whom was pierced,
the reason I now have sight

All seem to have agendas, fighting for rank, winning the daily war
I've seem to be left behind losing edge,
sometimes asking what's this all for?

The seas have risen once again, the flood
metaphorically speaking, the end
There's hidden truth to his lies spoken, these
foes all around we call friends

The beast arises, awakens, he comes forth
peering, looking within my eyes
Instinctively he sleepwalks through the
corridors, whispering softly he lies

Questioning him constantly always looking
around his shoulder, paranoia
Trying to fill in the void with another
addiction, substance to avoid her

He's releasing his most inner thoughts; she
listens to his words flow of tongue
Remembering all of his past transgressions,
fleeing from his fears on the run

They cannot be in the same room without
comfort, he hides within his quarters
His living space, the bed of lies, where he
stole her soul, still he supports her

My mind races with thoughts of unheard
crimes of the past, I'm sickened
How could one do such things to another?
The pace slowly rises and quickens

He gets things off his chest slowly, she
fights to remember conversations
Her memories fit like puzzle pieces with his,
remembering past reconciliations

He's one of them, programmed what to look
    for, the files of his heart discovered
His nerves start to creep up hard upon his
    shoulders like his yoke and blunders

Mishaps of yesteryear, the damage has been
    done, both old and young at fault
What's been done cannot be disassembled;
    the cost is as high as the assault

Trust is all but gone, disappeared, lost and
    forgotten, the song plays on repeat
He cannot crack the code held within the song,
    the lyrics, feeling low with defeat

Waking in the middle of the heaviest of sleep,
    the chorus, the choir starts to sing
Peace is filled in the room with the Holy Spirit,
    fit for only a prophet we call king

He's jittery and uncomfortable; the habit is
    fed with substance abuse to cure
He never can be wrong, he awaits the story
    unfolding before his eyes, he adores

The paths of the wood, there lays the hidden
    truths, deceit smelled only by dogs
For where filth is found you'll find flies and
    rot, memories shattered and clogged

He fears what's in the room, the demons call
    out him by name, mocking him
What and where does this disease come from,
    where is the root and the stem?

Trusting only a few, the pages turn slightly
left to right, up forward in disarray
Disoriented he walks in the shadows, he has
no organization of what might or may

The numbers are staggering, he holds onto
this life as if hell awaits him soon
For he cannot forgive mostly himself, so he
sleepwalks through the day and moon

He approaches the alter as the adolescence
comes forth from the pews
They reach out to touch the garments of the
father, the saved are the very few

Judged are his actions, demons fill his head,
consume his body and mind
Delusional his thoughts, he's confused, some
say he's a demon; others say he's kind

The pieces now fit together; trying to fit the
circle to the square is unreasonable
For the past is what leads to the present, controlling
the past making the future feasible

Though the future is out of sight and mind, it's
just a split second away from creation
For in God's eyes there is no blunder, for he
chastises, makes new this nation

For the perfect storm started with a bang,
now he calls home all he has created
So friend ask yourself these questions; where
are we going now, why are we sedated?

The answer lays within you and I, the night
starts and ends with a new call
Though I'm stricken with what man would
call sickness, I fight this fight for all

Stoppage of Time

November 15–16, 2017

There aren't any stars beyond this point, for there isn't any air
The cosmos fail to exist; there aren't any explosive forces to compare

There's a wall of nothing, there is no beginning or end
Only a stoppage of time, failing to be, neither foe of friend

Neither light or darkness comes forth, there just seems to be
The starting point from the place where you left both you and me

We are on a flat surface called a dimension, an illusion if you may
There isn't a center to it all, we spread apart and never stay

Always on the move, galaxies like dots amongst the cosmic line
All in the palm of his hand, insignificant
beings with purpose, designed

Dark matter, light, planets, stars, all facets
of life, elements wiped away
All our hopes and dreams seem without
meaning, beyond nothing lay

Imagination ceased to be, rain, sun, nothing
has traveled past this point
For the edge of the universe is in the fold,
bent like our lives clairvoyant

Thunderstorms of summer, planets born, stars exploding in space
Relativity is all but gone; there is nothing,
no winner or loser of the race

The end is where it starts, within reality lays the dimensions within
For heaven's entrance lies right there before us, let him carry you in

Finite to the creator like a pin on the needle,
threading, sewing the cloth
Mending us back together, making us
whole, new, obeying his own law

Dust and particles go forth into the nothing,
it is for our own well-being
For what has expanded billions of years
will collapse, faith is believing

Fold back together, if willed by him in a blink of an eye we'll see
For his wisdom is beyond measure, it's
infinite, all bend down to a knee

Though our home is infected, the universe is quarantined from sin
For once we lived hundreds of years, now
cancer runs rampant within

Like a ripple on the pond, it seems so vast, unreachable, so serine
In an instant the process starts its journey,
traversing through time not seen

Where is the end, where can we break
through? I'm worn from the fight
This day brings forth holy hours and
moments, it starts with a silent night

The size and vastness of space couldn't
add up to a particle of his being
For he's beyond the measurement of material
he has manifested so keen

Edges roughed out by the running waters,
        making us smooth on the surface
I'm jagged in heart, body, mind, and soul; I'm stuck in this crevice

The end to the beginning to everything in
        between marking the heavens
This is where I want to be for eternity,
        watching sunsets rise and leaven

The other side intrigues me, I'm curious to know if it's just a mirror
        A window looking into my eyes under the
                surface, again I could see her

Does dementia swallow up our existence
        like black holes within our world?
Making us children once again, I seem lost
        in the thick of things, the fold

Billions of galaxies lay all around us, unseen,
        untouched; the sea is unknown
There are parts of our own world unexplored;
        webs of lies are instead sewn

I don't belong here anymore; I've worn
        out my welcome in this town
I've traveled all but in a circle spinning, I leave never staying around

I pray with fervency to move on to the
        next part of my journey in life
In my mind there's more I can offer in some
        other place, it cuts like a knife

Does that place exist on the side unexplored, can I get there tonight?
        Is there any freedom from hate beyond what
                we see, two wrongs don't make a right

Here they cut you down, their words
weapons like sharp tongues, swords
Blood cold courses through their blackened
veins, marching all as one in accord

It now seems unfeasible, unobtainable to
achieve what once seemed so real
For light years have passed a whole life time,
my heart has been given to steal

For the taking, mongrels, thieves, and wolves
come to feed upon my flesh
Breaking my existing body down without
any repair, there's nothing left

Solitude is my medicine, my cure, to be on
my own adding a log to the fire
Burning incense to the heavens above,
there you won't find a single liar

My home is amongst the sick, the poor,
mentally insane, and the broken
For in this den of thieves I found nothing but
arrogance, the truth now spoken

I pray tonight my God will answer me, for
I want to go back home and be
Amongst whom and what I am and cannot
change, for I'm blind and cannot see

The Yoke

November 16, 2017

Hearts open wide to cut down, bleeding, deep pain
Trials amidst the salt of the waters, all but in vain

Separated by heavy chains, burdens, mostly fears
Taken into custody, tortured, beaten, shedding tears

Descending like a dove upon the earth, gentle rains
What was once lost now found, I've taken the blame

For the yoke falls upon my shoulders, plainly one sees
My fists bleed striking the walls of my prison I try to flee

Raped by a man, never seen or heard from again
Left there intoxicated and poisoned, nothing is the same

Revealed most eyes haven't seen, the wind calls him back
Returning to where it all began, remembering what he lacks

In the woods is where he lost his innocence, forced to watch
Looked upon what one so young shouldn't see, never forgot

Strong drink slowly fills the belly of the wicked
Memory erased from death inhaled, these are the inflicted

Hiding in closets, his bedroom left behind so fragile, young
Sleeping with white noise forgetting past, sweet songs sung

Oversexed children, forced to watch while they play
We can't change the channel in time, this is just the way

Yet I am the culprit, my hands tied and behind my back
It's my fault once again; I take all blame for the violent acts

Manipulated for pleasure, we seem to like to be played
Vulgarity of men upon women, into bed they are swayed

Where is love upon these shores of Normandy? Is there only war?
Where once there was sunsets, sparkling water be the seashore

For we've stormed the beaches, shot upon as target practice
Looked into the enemy's eyes from afar, listen to plans and tactics

The blame falls not upon of fathers but ours only, my friend
For the blame is directly upon me, now I must make amends

We stoned women of the past for transgressions of their sin
These same laws apply to both man and woman, all kin

Yet the burden, yoke lay upon my shoulders, sweltering heat
For the beam in my eye I must remove before I take the seat

Softly spoken promises, deceiving the prey, luring her close
Another trophy in the case we proclaim, and we boast

Yet the child watches from the bush, images last a lifetime
He crosses the bridge, oncoming traffic, ignoring the signs

The wars continue on, fought by men ignorant to the cause
Yet the blame lay upon my shoulders, I am not above the law

Is there true love upon these shores, this land we inherit?
Seems we've raped our way across continents, sadly I say it

We're all susceptible; we cannot ignore the truth at hand
Though what is real is sometimes ugly, brothers form a band

Yet I'm to blame, I have sinned, I take this yoke and task
I will conquer, no putting out the flame, I will take off my mask

Chill of the Night

November 17, 2017

She falls asleep tears stained eyes, pillow in hand
Alone she'll be tonight, though the break of morning comes

He sits there contemplating, distractions fill a small space
Otherwise compiled of anxiety, and escape seems unlikely

He closes the door; separate they make their ways and part
Tonight seems will last a lifetime, the
night echoes through the house

The excitement ends on the drop of a hat, normalcy takes over
The day changes mild, to rain, to sun covered rainbow skies

The songs call out in lighted room, the light never goes out
Hours spent in hope of his arrival, she closes the door, rests

Frustration fills my inner core; I sometimes force the words to flow
Anticipation of another story to tell,
wanting the entire world to know

Quiet is the room, my consciousness in and out, my breathing slows
My heart I wear on my sleeve, unable to take criticism, childish

The fog reaching over the waters giving way to the chill of the night
The blowing winds, clouds chasing east, give way to the stars

I wait upon our next meeting, what will be said, any significance
My prison awaits me, I feel the corner brings forth its inevitability

It's either this chair or the chair around the circle, stories told
Seeming the only respect I receive is from the broken, the poor

In the room I make my bed, I tidy up what little I have, I'm free
Though locked up behind doors of steel,
I'm free in the given moment

She lays there tonight, for whatever reasons she has, contemplating
I cannot forgive myself, the blame is set upon me, I cannot breathe

Suffocation, choking on the smoke of the raging fires of my past
The long road one should never walk, the call, heavens answer

I give all I have to God and to her, I owe this much to her suffering
She lays her head upon the pillow with tears, I pray she rests

The shell of the man I once knew is fading, he hasn't given up
At least not yet completely; he feeds himself courage to move on

The evening seems to journey on without any avail, motorist pass
I have nothing left to offer in that place, I've outworn my welcome

The start of my time, it all has but been stretched beyond measure
Psychological warfare has been the game since the very beginning

The visits have broken me down, yet I'm part of the flock, sickened
The stays though stretched out have been meaningful, I'm stronger

Today the keys await me, my trials continue, time has drawn close
I mustn't abandon my God, for he never left my side through it all

They have silenced the weak, they have medicated the prophets
Keeping what is truthful at bay, I take a stance against the wicked

Shall I continue to hide in the shadow or come forth, revealed?
Amongst giants I must conquer only by the strength much greater

Beyond the measure of any mortal man,
I walk unafraid, hand in hand
As in one accord with the gatekeeper, the master of the flock

My tomorrow is the very moment I live in from now until the end
The sick have spoken my name, told me who I am; here I am

I have come for one purpose alone and that is to testify, give witness
The children are godless; their god is science, technology of man

They believe on good works alone one will enter the kingdom
A kingdom that may or may not exist in
their eyes, only by convenience

Children are breed to serve the beast, to deny the Savior entirely
She sleeps soundly in the room unaware of my concerns, I pray now

The sun comes up over the ocean in the
east; the front chases its glow
The change has been slow but gradual, now the time has come

The door has shut for a season once again;
I'm left with artificial sound
Reminded of what there is and what is
when it comes around once more

The proof is in the silence of the night, the chirping of the crickets
It's in the storm that brings forth water for the crops, photosynthesis

Insanity is my everyday existence, my
companion, enemy, and my foe
It gives me meaning a hope to go forth
to goals set, I can be irrational

I'm spontaneous, my thoughts I seem I
cannot take hold of, I'm weak
Feeling stagnant, feet stuck in cement, unproductive, truth I seek

My cries come from the barren desert
waste lands, life flourished once
The cycle goes on by the hand of God, he reaches out to me

I've seen a tear shed in the cutting of the tree, his hand guides me
The hot days approach, the winters seem
to last a life time, storms brew

Vices I seek in order to forget reality, my pain, an escape I search for
The cold eyes lay all around me in the darkness, it now is my friend

I'm guided, rejuvenated by the serenity of the night, the stars above
They shine forth like an innumerable
amount of countless light bulbs

Flashes across a blackened canopy, only
made possible by his perfection
No man or angel could ever create such
beauty, paintings across the universe

For measurements and knowledge given to
man by the fallen are not theirs
It was never theirs to own, for it was brought
forth into existence well before

From the very creation, the plans were held
by the creator, cutting knives
Cutting knives, the thieves that feed upon
poor souls, souls stolen by the enemy

The sorrowful ways continue until the early
morning, hope brought forth
Light giving way, the bitter cold takes place wiping away all disease

Days spin out of control, the light seems to
give off anxious feelings, disgust
Winds howl every direction, waves form,
crashing upon the shore, eroding

The houses aligned by the waterfront highest
in value, the furry of the ocean
Taking no prisoners, the beating of the waters
rise without anyone to answer to

The ocean currents move just as she sleeps,
without warning she awakens
Coming to his senses he continues on with
the day, praying for a distraction

He feels the medication run through his blood,
rushing to his head momentarily
It's gone as fast as it arrived, coming down,
balancing out, nothing's accomplished

The thoughts are reoccurring, continually I seek and do not find
The days stretch out to what seems years,
seems like I'm always last in line

The keys out of sync, yet I listen intently as the race winds down
Though sometimes skills I lack, I always
try to find common ground

The highs avoid me; while I sit back writing these twisted thoughts
The dark knight waits eagerly to strike, to
take back, though I've been caught

My words get in the way of my intentions,
my theories wild and free
Waiting to take back what is rightfully mine, hold on and you'll see

These moments I live for, I seem to be at
peace even when I'm scrambled
My mind runs through mazes with twists and
turns, I roll the dice and I gamble

Taking chances for once in my life, learning to knock, seek, and find
Looking for a treasure that lies within me,
loving too much is my only crime

A dreamer I may be as she lays her head
to rest on her pillow tonight
I am guilty of being a fool once again as I
continuously pursue and write

How many words can describe one,
something elegant and most true?
Gracefully you move freely without any
blemish, I'm such a fool for you

One day you might read this and ask yourself, could that be me?
If you don't know it's my heart bleeding,
crying out for you like an endless sea

Like an ocean spilling over the levies, crashing
waves I'm like a massive storm
Searching for the missing piece to the puzzle
to keep me sane, somewhat norm

Of course it's been you, my friend, my love;
I'll wait for you even upon death
For your embrace makes me quiver, shake
with joy, you're all there is left

Amongst woman you stand out, above and
beyond all whom cannot compare
You're the reason I've been searching all these
years, not to have you isn't fair

But such is life; I cannot say I haven't tried,
taken a chance, given my all
Though there's much more I can offer, and
I will, I will someday take the fall

For I've seen the truth in your eyes, you're
every love song I've ever wrote
You're heaven's angel, and second to God I'd
give my heart to thee and devote

So remember these words when things
get hard in the end, stay strong
It was you who got me through these last couple
years through your prayer; so, so long

The Slain Warrior

November 18, 2017

The slain warrior lies in a pool of blood gasping his last breath
Consciousness in and out, thoughts of a child emerge to memory

Why? He asks one last time, as he fall victim to the sword
A brother has ended his life, sewn together
formed by one God alone

Man ending his fellow kin's life, stealing away what waits for him
The call no mortal wants to hear or make
fallen warriors upon the field

The battle rages on, as the sickened lust of
blood quench the rulers thirst
All is no longer fair in war, when by the push of a button all ends

The game is rigged, hacked, the scheme
is in order; technology thrives
Limbs missing, bodies disfigured, families changed forever

Children grow up fatherless, rage fills their
hearts, the pattern continues
Boys take a knee in protest, ignorant to who is behind the curtain

The puppet master, chuckling upon the
sight of the division of a nation
The soldiers sent forth to the four corners of the world, forgotten

The soldier marches on to the beat of a
nation, self-righteous, unaware
Children sent forth to die, honorable deaths, insanity, I digress

Facial-recognition systems gathering information only to destroy
Dismantle what and who we feel are the enemy, we're delusional

The stings of scorpions now revealed by flight of the drone piercing
Striking what enemy we proclaim, making threats against nations

Distinguishing right from wrong is all
but forgotten, rules abandoned
The game is in the hands of spoiled
children, crying out for attention

We have gotten far too advanced for our
own good, writings on the wall
The future has come forth from the bowels
of the earth, spewing fire

The super soldier now in the making, feeling no pain he emerges
Created not for empathy, but for destruction
upon the maker's command

The soldier watches on cheering as his
brother is dismantled, taken down
The final stage and battle has arrived, slain brothers rot in the streets

The video-game hacker is now the soldier,
life is mere illusion in his eyes
The day unfolds, the night hides the hidden
truths; friend, the game is over

Upon Fertile Soil

Merry Christmas, 2017

The lights go up round about the space and time once more
The house is filled with cheer, she watches with wonder and adores

Grace is ushered unto this family of beauty, God's favor finds thee
For their faith is most unusually, in these hard times as may be

Togetherness round the house, the tree lights up with aglow
For our Lord wouldn't bypass their devotion, one truly knows

Sister's faces radiant, shinning, the times could not separate the two
For the faith planted like seed within their
souls, rare is this found true

Upon fertile soil planted; thorns, bristles, and rocks dispersed
Their parents instilled, gave something
precious that can't be reversed

She makes room in her soul, for something
much greater than herself
Nothing could compare to the treasure
she's found, no earthly wealth

This year is much different; they will share their house once more
Together on Christmas morning, one family bound, and no storm

Storms of life shall not prevail on this holy family, and one will see
Together this time of year is what matters
most, brought down to a knee

Playful her nature, I see a sparkle in her eyes, a twinkle if you may
One rarely holds these truths, chains are
broken, her faith never frayed

Dedication to her service is impressive, she serves without ceasing
For her heart is beyond measurement of
man, she is a voice of reason

I can only imagine her soul light up with cheer watching the classics
Rudolf, Frosty, Wizard of Oz and more,
she is amazing, most fantastic

The breaking of bread and wine round the
table of the Lord, our Savior
Listening intently to what is offered, bringing the fruits of her labor

Most would ignore the miracles, dismiss
them as mere myth or legend
Though she is most unique in her faithfulness
amongst all her brethren

Community comes together on this most
sacred time of year once again
Yet year round her faith shines like a
thousand suns, he does now send

Sending her forth, freeing her soul to become what she needs to be
Blossoming into the beautiful swan she
is, chasing a dream and to see

Faith without seeing, her heart tells the
story at hand, future most bright
For a child is born once again, hope is born on the darkest of nights

Celebrations will arise, Christmas cheer will be passed round table
Yet the light will never to extinguished in her heart, most aren't able

I've seen your heart, and your devotion; you go above and beyond
For those who need you the most you don't
let down, and they've found

Light at the end of the tunnel, a spark,
one couldn't put out the flame
For what you give to this broken world
is hope, one reason you came

So when times of the season may wear on
you most, you'll forever shine
This no one can take away, for you're
most unusual and beyond kind

For God never makes a mistake, this you must remember to be true
Your heart is pure, you give us all hope,
you are chosen amongst the few

Shadows on the Sidewalk

November 21st 2017

Lost in a sea of forgetfulness, a fortress crumbling down
I was there where you had left me to die; I'm lost now I'm found

When is enough, enough? The shadows on the sidewalk disappear
The sun refuses to shine forth upon our face; it's been the longest of
years

The winds gather from the four corners of the earth, we shall soon see
These final days and nights my fingers crack to the bone, fall down
to knee

The nights are easier, I'm in a daze, I'm not as anxious with fear
I live now for these moments of bliss, not ashamed to shed a tear

I want to leave for good, to run away off into the abyss, chasing sun
To a time and place no one will know but me, to be on the run

The fear pulls me under, the distractions bend time and space between
My sentence is the moments in the daytime, the light shines forth;
I'm seen

The winter's cold bitter touch, keeps me from venturing out amongst
the stars
I feel I'm stranded in a desert barren, lifeless lands, no water and so far

Distances grow us apart, yet our hearts will forever be conjoined
No river, ocean, or continent could separate our love that's been sewn

Forged in the fire that cannot be broken, for the swords sharpened blade
Is masterfully crafted by the smith gifted, by the most precious medals made

Impatiently I flip the page, skipping over lines important to the
grand scheme
Overlooking the nuts and bolts, the keystone, most importantly the
theme

Hunger fills their bellies, no place to rest their weary heads, their souls
For they've been walking through the desert valley weeks, young
become old

To find someone with a heart, time to give, reaching out a helping hand
Is like finding a true woman to hold close, trust, not building castles
in the sand

The journey starts from a safe place, seems no need to take a chance
a first
One day you'll look back with regret, knowing your life could've
been reversed

The journey's twists and turns sometimes give you second thought
to go on
You must fasten your belt, tuck in your shirt; wash your face before
it's all gone

The sun fades west; this one can always count on forever to be true
For the angle of its setting is important, it is life and death between
me and you

The note is in my hands to give, the choice is now mine to make alone
I must decide in these few short days, avoid hiding in a cave of stone

I'm tired filled with fear of rejection, fear of judgment by mere man
For in these final days my belly is tight as I must make my final stand

Now I finally know what it feels to be alone, having nothing to hold
For the warmth of another I'll never embrace, though I have a heart
of gold

The days bring forth addictions, to feel and be something I'm not
I wish I could get back to the beginning once more, troubles I've
forgot

The music moves on in sync with my thoughts, a course I must proclaim
For what once was lost is now found, no two or more are ever the same

Crumbling Sand/ Opposite Charges

November 29th 2017

Words cannot describe these feelings anymore,
they're too few of them to use
Foiled by false illusions, freedoms that do
not exists, all we do is abuse

Most nights I lay awake, awaiting something
invisible yet more real than life
He comes to take home his prize possession
the church and make it his wife

Time zones are mixed, she waits upon
shores thousands of miles away
Wishing upon stars set high upon the midnight
sky, he comes without delay

Electricity fills the clouds above, opposite
charges intermingling with the ground
below here under heavens sky lightening
strikes, all can hear the sound

The trumpets blast, the coming has come and
arrived, patiently I await the call
for upon this less than solid ground I at times
falter, sometimes I can even fall

We've inherited the earth as a gift, souls
filled with both hatred and love
Polar opposite the forces all together, yet given
as freedoms from the one above

We have a choice to make my friend, together
fall or hold each other by the hand
If we choose the first of both we just might
stumble, crumbling with the sand

Overly sensitive to the fact that it kills him deep within and inside
Hoping all of his gray skies will clear, clouds will all step aside

They seem to just linger there without any purpose but to damper
Put a mode of distress, giving fear, doubt,
sometime misery all around

The night now is silent, sounds once
bustling with life faded with time
The sleep has taken over the circle of life, there
seems to be no rhythm or rhyme

The lights upon the tree help me fade away to places of serenity
As I rest my head upon this pillow my
eyes, my mind drifts away slowly

The end seems all too near upon this soul
filled with paranoia, exhaustion
I pray she understands this foolish man, I
seem lost and cannot find love

I had it once, it was extraordinary, it lit a fire burning brightly inside
I couldn't hold back my excitement, my joy,
on my sleeve worn, I couldn't hide

I don't want to waste anyone's time, I'm
complacent where I am unfortunately
Stagnant are my days, wonder has left my
heart, my feelings turn to ash

I avoid my sickness altogether, avoiding
pain, wishing just to feel ecstasy
Yet it avoids me at all cost, I just seem to be, exist without feeling

Temporary thoughts of somehow controlling
my fate, or having false security
Pressing without prayer, greed and arrogance
fill the heart of the sinner

The offsetting of both the dosages give
way to another me once again
Who am I now, am I coming or going, is this
me? I wish to lend out my hand

The pages seem to stay stuck with time without him even noticing
A reminder of what he needs to work on,
his prayer, unselfish venting

Asking forgiveness not just for himself but
for his transgressions against others
Knowing there's hope because he once came
for all, both for him and his brothers

Words flowing off the page, blankly I stare off
into a nearby corner deep in thought
My head filled with irrationality, forming false
sense of insecurities, I'm vulnerable

I pray my heart can be worn upon my sleeve
once again, there for the taking
For just to feel one last moment, bringing
my to tears, is my one last wish

To feel heartache again would tell me I at least
had tried, it would be well worth it
To kiss her lips tender, to lock eyes passionately,
this is my prayer this evening

The effort I have put in must wear off, I feel
God will supply me with the tools
The tools necessary to at least have one last
go around, dancing with my fate

This Day

December 1st 2017

Opening the window to the eyes of the soul,
exposing one's inner most thoughts
This day was made in history's past, lingering
on like a thorn upon a rose

Blaming himself for the past, leaving all he
ever had to die, forgetting family
He was too young to make such rash decisions,
radical and narrow minded

His focus was primarily himself alone, furthering
his case to be relaxed, complacent
Laziness would get the better part of him most
his life, drugging himself to forget

Dismissing the very truths that haunted him,
allowing him to server false gods
Mixing toxins and potions together to
become something entirely different

He's afraid to let in what might strike back with
vengeance, tearing apart at the seems
Payback two fold for what he has done, soon
he will face down the demons

What has he created, a monster that is soulless,
reckless to the point of no remorse
Glorifying a mix of deadly thoughts of vile
so inappropriate, cold is his blood

Crawling upon the ground, tasting the dirt
of the earth, choking upon the ashes
This day is not like any other, it's a continuation
of what could have been destroyed

Yet was allowed to be brought into life, existence
as it may be, others killed before him
Three persons to be exact in number, silenced
by laws of this governed land

Her body lay in shambles, never the same her
life would be, the drug breaks the vein
What if's and could have been is what her
life has most consisted of, broken

This day is just a reminder of what has
manifested since the beginning of time
An evilness lurks in the shadows tonight, he
waits filling his belly with the waste

The vices and addictions add up surmountable
beyond any count made by man
He suffers now with his conscience, sleep he
has no more, the pill has destroyed him

No longer does he allow the images to creep
up into the rear-view, he speeds away
Distancing himself to immeasurable amounts,
miles upon miles left behind

Forgiveness and penance is his life, once in
defiance of his father and his request
His guidance avoided by turning a blind eye,
ignoring the signposts and the symptoms

Lost within these chambers, this prison cell,
these walls thick with resentment
Most would forget, dismiss their own conduct,
move on without hesitation

Though he walks aimlessly in the dark, the back
of his mind the curse won't go away
He has done his time and sentence, the next
stage is set for him, he must go on

The day another reminder of what venom still
lingers on, his followers on his heels
Traps have been set before him, trusting
nothing because of the manifestation

The coming together of evils, witnessing what
once was just a small sin at hand
Now out of control with furry and rage, the
cancer takes hold of the patient

Exhaling is now the only thing in mind, for
breathing takes upon contamination
The filth of the air we breathe is appalling and
unacceptable, we must not forget

How can the destructiveness of such a man
meet the loving arms of the same?
Flipped is the point of view, the door seems to
be always shut because of his shame

He seems to forgive neither himself or any
other, setting the standard in the mirror
On the flip side the left is the right, and neither
no what the other is doing at any time

Mimicking each and every move until the
very last deed done, exhaustion arises
The choices have caught up with him, now
he lives a life of remorse and shame

The day is like no other, for now time as
halted, it has come to the crossroads
A place where the fork hits the road, either
root will lead him to certain torture

For he has forged in the fires and pits of
abomination vileness so insurmountable
Those unaccounted for wait for the return, the
coming back of a king without a crown

For he who has been made from both honey
and vinegar shall come together as one
Once again shall he reign, this time given one
last chance, for this day is like no other

Split Into Kingdoms

December 9th 2017

Four corners point and lead to the center of the room, it's empty
No doors to escape the pain deep inside, the day bleeds into the abyss

Confusion upon the day, the hour, the time, persistence overcomes
For those who answer to the one true Lord on high win out the day

The prison awaits in the shadows, the time isn't too far into the future
Now the moments blend together mixing to gray then black canopy

The canvas once white in color now burst open with color of abundance
Hope is born again to a door that has been opened to the few believers

He sits in peace knowing peace resides in the bedroom down the hall
Finally she can sleep soundly knowing the direction of the tides changed

The music of the season plays all around, this year is much different
He feels at peace if only for a moment knowing there's work to be done

The winds gather from the corners of the earth, the storm winds prevail
Once a land mass formed by the hand of god, now split into kingdoms

Majesties formed by human possessions of gold and silver, one ring to rule
Their thoughts blinded by deceptions so devious in design, tainted

As the circle spins in space the stars and galaxies repel away in disgust
Once closer holding onto what was true and sincere now laying down arms

The rescue and life boats have been let down, yet the passengers outnumber
There's not much time for backup, I look upon heaven to come down

The daylight is about to break, I must now enter a place of anxiety
For these pills take away what is true about me, I'm better off in the dark

The snow from the west slowly approaches, beauty the smell, silent sounds
The drive I take out into the early evening morn, car lights slowly pass

Please Lord let this be true for me, I haven't had this great a feeling
So long have I awaited yesterday, Our Mother looks down upon me

Please ask your son to watch over me, allow me to make a difference
A change for him, in his name, never to give up as long as I have you both

Patience I will learn, my time is now, and with you in my corner I'm free
Though the night can feel long I take pleasure in knowing there is peace

My solitude is my closest alliance, my friend and my co-conspirator
We plan together with the prayers of the saints what comes next

The journey may be long, but with the blessings of heaven there is hope
My soul is trapped within this body and mind, it is my internal torment

I cannot escape this flesh that burns and is torturing seemingly every moment
Back and forth the angels fallen and in heaven battle within my being

I must ride out the storms of life, and journey through the bowels
of hell
Then and there shall I take back what belongs to my Lord, the lost
souls

Souls that have been tormented, the time has come for them to come
home
They sing in unison asking for forgiveness, there tongs hot with thirst

The scraps of the table they would gladly accept, for just one more
chance
For now they are trapped within individual cells of hopeless days and
nights

But now the time has come for all that to change, the graves shall
open
Released for the battle at hand, the battle that has been foretold and
won

I've come to far to let this moment slip away, physical beauty is
fraudulent
I've seen what is underneath the garment, the flesh wears away to rot

What is real is the soul, I've seen souls so beautiful they outweigh
vanity
I see the bodies of the dark angel sway through the media into our
quarters

Demonizing our children, snatching away our morality, they never
seem to lose
Another way to make money, notes giving back upon interest, hidden traps

The fires of the west rise higher reaching the skies above with such
atrocity
What I have felt will never be reversed, just control and manipulated

Forged by the hands of the molder, the glassblower forms, twisting material
Shine full of colors plentiful, the potter waits patiently while his creation takes form

The planter waiting for the times of the season to come into play, rain and sun
Pouring washing down upon the earth in preparation of a new harvest

She feels his passion and so the quarrels of papacy begin from the very start
Hidden windows and agendas all but forgotten over the years to be settled

The sheep on the right, the wolves placed on the left whom devour innocence
Prowling over God's children, running through once green pasture now desolate

Running through kingdoms of old with treasures bountiful, presently barren
The tides have and will change now, horses and cattle once bound by chains

The Forgotten

December 8th 2017

The lost and the forgotten, their paths cross and intermingle once
again
Thousands of years in between they have suffered, seemed without
a friend

Chronic illness is their disease, yet the king comes down soon, will
arrive
All plagues will leave and disperse, for the weak not the strong will
survive

There is hope among the cursed, their bodies lay in shambles, left
behind
Children unable to fend for themselves, their birth is their only crime

Soon fire will rain from above, from a deceiver, born to lead the
world astray
The moment he will change to course of mankind, the truth, life,
the way

Patience is required, the mother knows the best way how, looking
on high
She whispers in her sons ear, I know a plan, it's secret, they laugh and
sigh

Bring him to the sick and lame, let him see what truly is going on
here
Show him what's behind the scenes, what he's turned a blind out to
in fear

The children sleep in their rooms, yet the underprivileged shall become one
They will carry on ways of truth and justice, for the saved will only be some

Most will fade into the night, but the graves shall be released with much joy
For the work of a king must be lowly to the world, he's reserved and he's coy

Our mother calls out to him from the desert, come here without any nourishment
You will be burned from the scorching sun, wipe away sin, gain encouragement

No longer will I fill the ego, I shall let the reward be god working through me
Let the children be my gold, so my soul and my days and nights will be set free

Too many hours have been spent banging my head against the wall in frustration
Now I must give back to whom truly deserves our respect, I sit in contemplation

I pray tonight this plea, this prayer will find heaven above, this is my letter
My prayer is sent up in an offering, a gift, this is all of me for worse or better

The demon was left to torment their days and their nights, they will soon rise
For smoke always comes up word offered as sacrifice without compromise

The letters are written, he shall be in check, though they will laugh and scorn
He must finally be free from his burdens of his own hell, for years he's been torn

I lay awake in a state of accomplishment, though my thoughts I hold to be tested
For my time here will not last for eternity, I'm mortal, now I must be invested

Giving all of myself to the inflicted, the poor, the blind, and the lame, forgotten
For they show us what life is really all about, though at times I may be softened

Yet in weakness I will find strength, made pure again for all to see, be proud
Though I will not stand looking for human praise, I will be silent among the crowd

For the meek will inherit the earth, the sick thought to be dead will be risen
From their graves they will rise, coming to life, gentle hands will lead them

Dry waste lands replenished by the cool rushing waters brought forth from springs
Land once dominated by landscapes of radiant color and beauty, the bell rings

Tolling at the end of ages for all to hear, rich, poor, and everything in between
Color holds no prejudice, the ends of the earth to the universe uncovered and seen

The essence of the moment is like no other, I've looked into the eyes of the wicked
I've seen their male intent, their motives, cruelty most unconventional, the afflicted

The heartbeats loudest when there is fear that consumes, our lies tell the story
For the grace of the one above exceeds all, he comes here in all of his glory

Please lord let me get this, I will prove your spirit can and will work through me
For it is your love that has healed this poor mans soul, the demons now will flee

For through my sickness you have given me grace, I am forever thankful to thee
My gift are these hands, this mouth, the instrument of love, I now kneel upon me knee

Struck by Lightening

November 28th 2017

Habits are formed from the knowledge of man or lack of
Seeming to out smart the enemy, ourselves, starting out as love

The planets distinctively retracted against the midnight sky
The atheists, fully unaware of what's to come, not ready to die

This pain we feel though temporary is redemptive indeed
So we mustn't think it's all in vain, that God would take up and leave

The moon sets once again over the waters calmed from the storm
The winds have howled for weeks, once forgotten, now the norm

The cold comes from the north, making its presence felt early
I pray she's right around the corner, so maybe we could spend eternity

She prayed for me tonight, to be more warm and receiving
To open my eyes to the one true God and start again believing

Days can lead to nights of distress, though he leads us home again
Sometimes things feel they take a lifetime, like finding a friend

Someone to confide upon, praying most every night with tears
Fighting for what's right, for the strength to overcome all our fears

Late at night my angel comes a visits, waking me to go on and pray
For the time of the new day is at hand, on this couch looking up I lay

The lights flicker around the room, the music fills my heart and ears
Anticipation of the weekend enters my being, I cannot wait to see her

Will she see past the dirt upon my face, the scars upon my wrists
Looking past the years of guilt and remorse, this man's aging face

I doubt, I cry, I'm broken, yet my spirit is most alive and true
Seeing you where scarlet purple is most beautiful, and so are you

Could fate have brought me here to this point and beyond?
There's something bigger at hand in charge as I sing this love song

For love isn't what you see in the movies, it goes beyond vanity
For if it was perfect it wouldn't be true, it takes work and our sanity

We must hold each other close to our heart, for in numbers we succeed
We are told it to go alone, stay on your island, from truth we flee

Do let your heart be troubled of hardened, open up your arms to all
For the cuts you're about to receive are a must, now hear God's call

There's no use in hiding, you must expose yourself, heart upon sleeve
Cast aside all your fears, gaining inner strength, the past you must leave

I do not search for a crown or ring, money and wealth is not my goal
What I do search for is God in every eye, to never sell this poor soul

Give away all I have in my heart, my treasures to seek his face
The face of God where I'd fall to knee, erasing all time and space

For once someone real has shown me interest, someone whom shares
Common ground upon solid rock, someone whom truly cares

Fading west is what I'll do, it may take me all but an hour in prayer
Hoping it's all worth it in the end, into hazel eyes once again stare

The lame and sick shall enter the kingdom first and foremost
All else fall in behind like soldiers in certain rank, we mustn't boast

For the humble and the meek shall inherit the earth and God's kingdom
These truths I hold dear to my heart, this is what matters, our freedom

So from this moment I pray you rest well, that Jesus has your heart
You may or may not be the one, but God's children will never be apart

Stars Align

Christmas 2017

Though blue is in the sky above, your eyes are filled with life of green
Knowing you is something I do not deserve, yet though it may seem

I've fallen upon an angel, one whom belongs among the highest of heights
A gift from heaven given to us all, wiping all wrong away making right

Your faith is strong indeed, I've seen your strength come alive inside
Cages couldn't hold back the truth you possess, your love is so alive

Holding your hand in prayer is surreal, talking for hours upon end
Knowing I can confide in you so, I will do all in my power that I can

To make you realize I'm true, my heart bleeds with God's presence above
It is because of him that I have a second chance, it's because of him I love

The moment I saw you for the first time my breath was taken away
You got out of your car so graceful, hours passed wishing I could stay

Your smile is beyond measure, your voice pleases our Lord on high
There is no denying your dedication to Our Mother, above Angels sigh

Relief is what you give this fallen world, a brand new start to us all
For if it wasn't for a precious gift such as yourself, we'd truly all fall

We ran together in the park, I didn't mind waiting for you to catch up
For just to be by your side was good for me, it was definitely enough

I know what you have been through, I have felt the pain many nights
Wishing all of it could be taken away, knowing that we have to fight

We must stay strong, we are part of the chosen few, I feel it in my bones
If you ever need someone to lean upon, know you'll never be alone

For I am at your side, I will fight for you, you mustn't ever forget
We have been brought forth to meet and be strong, he is our safety net

I sat alone that night, the space was there for you to take if you may
Just a couple hours is all I needed to believe, the music that we played

The years have brought forth much pain, but my faith has remained
firm
I see the same within your eyes, I wish to pick you apart and learn

I pray the stars will align in heaven on high, raining grace upon thee
For just one moment in your arms I would melt, for with his strength
I see

The time spent with you went by too quickly, waiting for our next
meeting
Is like waiting for eternity to go by, I cannot wait until your greeting

With the moonlight gathering, forming the night's glow upon your
face
Sunshine cannot hide in the darkness in your presence, stopping
time and space

The stars and cosmos above gathering together, pairing, therefore
giving light
Nothing could stop or take away from your beauty, not even darkness of night

The years couldn't stop or take away, and time cannot erase or destroyed
For what you've come here to accomplish will be done and not left void

Loving and caring, patient with others are just a few gifts among plenty
For what God placed in your heart from the beginning holds, you give sanity

Balance to life is crucial, separating yourself from what could and may destroy
For knowing the difference of what can and cannot be done, this you can't avoid

Seems the answers are getting harder each day, but within us the answer is revealed
For God shines forth his grace and his light among his people, to him we kneel

My thoughts are with you this evening, wondering what you're dreaming about
What dances through your mind in your sleep, to the heaven's I acclaim and shout

Sweet hymns and praises we give to the highest upon high, yet in comparison
Your shinning face gives light to the world, the pages flow without halt as my pen

Scrambling to take down what is needed to be said, your eagerness is forefront
Your power coming from God's throne, rushing waters couldn't stop the currents

Whirling round and about, tossing like waves upon the sea, you calm the storm
For the strength of a thousand suns couldn't compare, you're out of the norm

So when it's time for us to be called home, your mansion in the sky awaits
While my tiny tent in heaven is in no comparison to thee, this is sure fate

For you're a gift to not just this world, you're a gift to your church and to me
I thank the lord god up above for leading me to you to the heavens I decree

John The Baptist

December 12th 2017

From the belly of his mother he leaps with
joy at the presence of his lord
Shouting out from the desert make straight the
path of one whom comes with a sword

A blade of love, every lasting life in abundance,
his glory shall and will not ever end
To the ends of the earth his work shall be
proclaimed, making enemies friends

Going out eating just locust and honey, he awaits
the coming day that's been foretold
For he baptizes with holy water, yet our lord
comes baptizing with fire most bold

The forgotten years of John were lost, his story
is on the back burner say to least
For all eyes were set upon the king of kings,
though John was the chosen priest

His father dumb in speech, his mother promised
a son whom shall not take strong drink
For he must stay sober each and every moment
for the king, for he shall not blink

For in the eyes of a child we see the spark and
fire which comes firing out within
Though John had his faults and failure along
the way, the king of kings did not sin

I would imagine when they were young, they
would spend the days and nights together
Looking upon the same skies above, going through
trial, one day they would be forever

In the kingdom looking down and praying for
both you and me, wishing upon a star
The one rising in the east brightly shinning
brighter than all others in the distant so far

One day he would be arrested, put in jail, liars
and thieves would put him to death
For the request of the dancer would be deadly,
now regret is all the king had left

Herod promised her foolishly that she could have
whatever she well pleased and requested
For the mindless act of strong drink and persuasion
of the girl, Herod would be tested

Johns head would be put on a platter, displayed
for the world to see, it is but a shame
For his passion for the one to come after him
exceeded all, he never looked for fame

Jesus wept when he heard the dreadful news,
the day and night must have been long
John would die a martyrs death, for his fate was
by the sword and from his lips the song

His crying out in the desert was not all in vain,
for the followers were well aware
Jesus would follow shortly behind this baptist,
into each others eyes they would stare

For if it wasn't for him coming out to proclaim,
the deaf and forgotten would never be
John whom was missing from Jesus's final days
shall never be taken away from you and me

Part 2

Tale of Twelve Days/ Within My Own Prison

The Tale of Twelve Days/
One Year Later
My Diary

August 15–26, 2017

Unsteady heart, whispering sounds from
the forest, the night is young
Wondering what she's thinking now;
I ask, what now will I become

The future though uncertain, I know all
is in his tender gentle hands
Tonight I rest in his arms wide open, feeling
lost at sea I search for land

I doubt, I fear, I'm ashamed of my status
in comparison to this world
I've made excuses all my life; I need
assistance from above, intersession

Do the losers ever win? Will I get my day
in the sun? Every day I fight
On this holy day Our Mother assumed to
Heaven giving me grace and sight

I nervously look up to the stars, wishing
upon the first one I see shine high
Heavens' height beyond comprehension of
man, he's true never telling a lie

I've waited for these moments for plenty a
time, working hard, not giving in
These years at times have been a struggle,
torturous nights standing still

Wearing my heart on my sleeve, giving,
never asking anything in return
I have absolutely nothing left inside besides
the Holy Spirit; I'm clean and burned

He sways me to tell the truth, the inner
workings of this world strangle hold
On our youth sickened with the horror of
lies, sex, brought into the fold

The children are stained, their eyes filled
with hatred, testing the waters
Crying out from below the surface, rising
tides, expecting not respectful

What was once clean is now distorted; the
garden tainted the purity of hearts
Indulgences, never having enough, never
knowing the truth from the start

Once they believed without question, they
saw his face, but were led astray
Looking upon the cross with awe, running
into the Father's arms without delay

Stranger came into their lives, deceit now
lingering upon the fragile minds
Impressionable and malleable nature torn,
never again will they ever find

The excitement of a seashell, listen to the
ocean within, golden sun setting
Hearing the words of our Savior speaking
to his children, opening the book

The feel of the pages stuck upon the finger,
watching the story come alive
Abraham, Moses, David, and more—our
reason to live, honor, give, and strive

The wicked brought and stricken down by
the wrath of the Lord up on high
A country and king so stubborn moving
his troops across the sea parted

The stories mean so much, relevance to our
modern day world beyond belief
The recognition is sadly forgotten, put on
the back burner, a side note a best

He comes like a thief in the night, the candle
is lit, the oil in the lamps is low
Be ready for the bridegroom, my friend, stay
alert and pray and you'll bestow

He comes in the silence, his light burns
bright in the darkest of all crevices
There is no place to hide; tunnel, cave, in
the cover of night all is revealed

My mind wondering down memories lane,
wishing upon what I once had
She's far across the universe, wishing upon
another star, I'm all but forgotten

I left my heart with her; I can't seem to love
again, lusting over forbidden fruit
Beauty only on the outside, soulless beings,
emptiness inside I follow suit

I plead and ask for forgiveness, sins repeating,
hypocrisy fills my wasted days
The evil one watches me filling me with
lies, telling me I'm illegitimate

I ache with inner fear, believing in the
poisonous venom that enters my veins
Even calling it comfort and healing, my skies
filled with colors which are stains

The celebration goes on, swaying silhouettes
in the shadows, unfaithfulness
Trust is all but lost, talk is even cheaper; sparks
create the raging fire now bright

The inferno of hell fire never goes out, though
here the ambers glow slow, dim
The night bird sings one last song, slow,
elegantly moving in the night sky

The fireflies and forest fill with summer
sound, the silent night embraces life
I sit upon the shore, my seat a log once
planted so high upon the earth fertile

I look out upon the waters calm, alone,
thinking of what I know I cannot have
She's taken; the enemy has won her over
momentarily, knowing my weakness

Shooting stars telling the time and the seasons
past, present, future, I'm in awe
Riches of this world couldn't compare to the
awesomeness of what's to come

I feel him in the warm sun on a cool brisk
autumn's afternoon, light slow breeze
I the stillness of the night, the owl upon its
perch; sounds of song touching ear

Will I ever be content? Will I ever be satisfied
with my accomplishments, few
Will I just compare myself to this world? A
failure to my peers, obscuring view

My body is failing me, my legs cannot keep
up with my goals, I'm falling behind
My writing a rant, my writers block setting
in, I approach the four corners sign

This waiting is killing me, I'm tired but
cannot sleep; rest avoids my being
Nothing is ever good enough, I'm lost at sea,
sun beating down, without cover

Explosions in the night sky, blue, green,
radiant while I watch from the shores
The stars moving ever so slightly, marching,
while planets resists pulling back

She enters my mind again; I cannot seem to
let her go, ripple in the water stirs
It pulses, navigating outward like the universe
expanding, dying; reverting back

I walk alongside the two lakes, searching
anyway to meet together, no barrier
One side rough current, crashing waves, the
other silent, calm sparkling mirror

Night and day, like my soul torn between
right and wrong, seeking a balance
Black and white fill my days and nights, never
grays or in-betweens, nor silence

Simple is what I seek, complication my best
friend, companion, yet foe, enemy
The straight and narrow path lights the way,
yet crooked, twisted, thorn and root

Choking the seed, growing on the path without
fertile ground, scorched by sun
My eyes blinded by truth, raped by my inner
most desire, I start to flee and run

I look for someone, something to lean upon,
other than my faith, and faith alone
I cannot do this by myself I say, the crowd is
gathering violently looking to stone

Killing my soul, my inner being, my wealth
accumulated, measured by my talent
Talents earning my only praise from
acquaintances, nothing less than valiant

Though I was once lost now I'm found, my
mind is sick and acceptance is lost
I cannot forgive myself, that's my biggest
defeat; I'm left counting all the cost

The moon soon will cover the sun, blocking
out all of its rays, darkening skies
Blinding the children here, eyes to burn, we
have all grown old and now all lie

Pointing the finger, laying blame, condescending,
making another feel obsolete
I ask myself, what is wrong with me? Why
am I so repulsive and unwanted?

Is it because I have nothing to give to another?
Am I a failure, lack of success?
Maybe she just wants security, and I'm just
poor, or maybe I'm just plain ugly

The days blend together, my eyes blurred
vision as I nod off, closing eyes
Tiredly drift away into the morning sounds,
white noise calming my senses

I press the keys like the pianists strikes the
cord, sounds softly tell the story
Use the language painting pictures unseen
by human eye, colors magnificent

The battle never ends; if it did the winner
would send his spirit down on me now
I need you, Lord, I'm dying inside, tears fill
my eyes, my wounds are exposed

My scars aren't fully healed; our hearts are
breaking tonight, am I the reason?
The reason why you're so patient waiting
for every piece of the puzzle to fit

My heart sinks low tonight, hands unsteady,
the night now draws to a close
The song is written, her answer is given, my
friend, there's a thorn to every rose

Darkened is the midday sky, moon eclipses
what brings forth life to sustain
I write with forewarning what's to come, the
sky tonight filled with the stains

Sun burning bright and large, starring into a
world of mere illusion and fiction
God knows the past, present, as well as the
future, his upper hand on the liar

The deceiver places doubt and fear; solutions
of pleasure are his only options
Now the resistance must become truth, the
intercession of Jesus and his mother

Prayers given by the father to the son directly,
my last friend will not give up
Praying for me is his final request; I'm finally
free from all tyranny, oppression

I wait sober now, in the cover of darkness and
shadow, hiding, waiting; watching
I hear the shrieking of their hell cries, burning
ready to wage war with heaven

The battles have been fought; the losses have
piled up; now the real war begins
A war that has been settled since the beginning
of time, the sword set to strike

In his mouth the sword is held steady, words
ready to tear apart the competition
Kings and queens gather together from the
ends of the earth, fall upon their knees

He comes upon the clouds up high, a throne,
a chariot, the world blinded by light
Two in a field, mother and child, separated
by rapture, the trials now are at hand

Tribulation is in full effect, death, disease,
war, famine; brought by two witness'
The world blaming them for their destruction
given power from above on high

Our sins have caught up with us, giving ourselves
out of wedlock, killing innocence
Pleasure has been our new god, excess drinking;
accepting sin without morals

The moon now bloodred, the sun blackened
out, the stars tossed from the heavens
Skies painted by stain, filled with infestation,
boils on our bodies, hoping for death

Death we shall not receive, only suffering, we
now have left God behind; we're alone
Our arrogance, cut throat words, attacking
each other with hatred, slitting throats

For now the night goes on, an hour left until
the new day begins, time has ceased
The hour on the clock has stalled, the hands
fail to turn; the dates are set in stone

Constellations move through the night sky;
they're watching in observatories intently
Angels are approaching at the speed of light,
ready to make their final stand

The air saturated with dampness, hard to
sleep, the streets cluttered with traffic
The white noise never subsides, city lights in
the distance, exhaust of the tail pipes

The dark side of the moon revealed, the diamond
glow and ring, the hour has come
The music will soon be gone forever more,
the satellite creeps along the horizon

He tells me, do not be afraid! I have overcome,
rule the world, and I have conquered
Conquered death, won the war before time
was brought to light, I call you friend

Peace is my gift I give to you; hear my soft
words seep into your soul this evening
Though I leave you soon, the peace I leave to
you will reside, Holy Spirit come forth

Though presently you feel you cannot face
this task, nor take the yoke upon you
You shall prevail; you shall speak to kings with
power and conviction, confidently

Prison doors will open upon request, I will not
leave you to die nor be made a fool
Words shall be given to you in defense; they
shall know I am Lord above all creation

I am in charge of this place they call their
domain, they are fools, dust in the wind
Worms and rot upon the earth, their souls will
suffer my wrath, because I am the Lord

Prophets have foretold these coming days, wished
to be present amongst my coming
Written upon the stones of the world and the
ancient foundations, are these words

Languages from one end of the earth to another,
Tower of Babel shall be destroyed
My words have reached the ends of the earth,
time has stopped, and I'm coming

There are wolves dressed in sheep's clothing
amongst you, my friend, they're faceless
They're a farce, they make you out to feel
insignificant, worthless; they're liars

Watchful eyes are upon you, peering and
glancing over shoulder, spying cheats
Darkened eyes soulless, ready to pounce upon
you at any moment, digging dirt

You've made your bed, now you must face the
consequences, I will not leave you
You're surrounded, they're petrified of you;
they don't know what to make of you

The trials have now begun, they will try to
trap you, catch you in lies, manipulate
They fear you, they don't understand you,
think you're the enemy, they're wrong

I have protected you all these years, all this time;
the choice is now yours, my friend
There's only so much I can do, you must
use freewill, I know the outcome

Do not fear, the feeling is useless and an
illusion, your eyes will deceive you
Do not use your eyes, use the senses that I
have given you, intuition is your ally

The beautiful wear masks, they're part of his
plan to destroy, lead you to death
He will try to bring you with him to where
he knows he will spend eternity

The lake of fire awaits him and his orator,
messenger of false hope to the sheep
The lost sheep being played for fools, the chill
you feel on you back is my hand

My hand upon your shoulder, I give you rest
as the day comes to an end, I'm here
The songs you sing are my words, my inspirations,
my warnings, encouragement

What you've written is a manuscript, show this
to the world and be torn to shreds
The countdown has begun, the time is at
hand, are you ready, they're watching

Mistakes upon error, the day stretches forth,
sun setting the night gradually arrives
Motion is set forward like a broken clock
slowly fading away, all night I drive

Looking for the treasure; a treasure left behind
years ago brought here in secret
The cup of blood, the cup of life, it runs
through veins intermingled, a hybrid

Letting sin take over his days, giving into hate,
the dark forces draw him in slow
His body and mind feel the pull of death,
grasping tightly onto what he holds onto

He cannot seem to let these thorns that stab
him go; they pierce his side so deep
The pull of sin sways him to repeat the cancerous
process, the drug runs and seeps

His mind and body cannot seem to rest,
relaxation avoids his nights and days
Knowing what is right and wrong is half the
battle, the reality is the bed he made

The pictures burn within his mind, photographs
and nightmares collide and clash
Moving images so enticing, hard to ignore,
everywhere you look he's bombarded

The night goes on; the day comes to a close,
the television plays, white noise
I cannot seem to let her go, she seems to push
me away, yet she acknowledges me

She thanks me for my kindness, my heart
melts, I'm in full gratitude, waiting
I wait for anything to interrupt my menial day,
giving me something to hold onto

Summer slips through my fingers like the girl I
had so close to my heart at one point
She is a woman of the stars, heavens angel, I
picture her as I do Mary, with respect

Respectfulness beyond all compare; she's a gem,
and the enemy has taken her away
I pray to my Lord Jesus, the Heavenly Father
above, to intercede, for her hand

Her hand to hold, cool to the touch, to warm
her by the winters fire, my heart aches
To kiss her lips, to draw her near, to smell
her skin, her hair, to feel her breath

He has taken her from me, tonight in frustration
I seem to settle for just images
Images of lust, fakeness, reality is mere illusion,
I pray not to give in and falter

I would protect her, keep her safe from all harm;
go to the ends of the earth for her
I would die for her, suffer for her, go the all
lengths and further beyond for her

Tonight I sit here alone, listening as the night
fades to tomorrow, I never sleep
I wait for him patiently; depression seems to
be my friend now, for I forever keep

I have all the time in the world, yet my body
is failing day by day, I'm fading
The day approaches when she will be gone;
no longer will she be there to talk to

Worry and anxiousness is prevalent now, it
soon will amplify beyond imaginable
Knowing she will be with those alpha male,
perverted monsters, sickens me

The enemy wears civilian clothes, and so does
our own, the blend together, unison
Their mindsets are the same; they have no
values, only their own twisted thoughts

Midnight approaches and it seems I've let
down myself and the world once again
When will you return? I repent, but continue
to fall, I ask for forgiveness for my sin

She comes to me in song, chanting her fair
name; please rid me of these crimes
My past is catching up to me; my present is
making me old, now is the time

Holy water wash away my inequities, I falter,
I fall daily, I ask for assistance
I seem to be alone in this world, my beliefs
seem to be mine and mine alone

All persons my age have left the beautiful
church; they go to tickle their ears
Fill them with things they want to hear, heaven
isn't cheap, my friend, God I fear

Their prayers give me hope, the chase intervene
giving the lay hope, encouragement
The midnight hour comes forth like a thief in
the night, encompassing development

What are the true ways, confusion and doubt
fill my mind, information overload
I waste my time self-indulging, caught up in
my own desire, taking the high road

I come to the intersection, the four corners,
where to turn, should I go back?
Sometimes the hardest thing to do is to start
all over again, all my life I slacked

I'd like to think what they're saying is that
everything is going to be alright, fine
That the morning will bring promise, I won't
have to fear or doubt, crucify myself

I never give myself credit, I win battles; I do
things I never thought were possible
It's not good enough, I still put myself down;
rip myself apart, my soul incorruptible

Though it will go onto God knows where, my
body will turn to dust until resurrection
The night songs blend with the chanting, the
songs of the angels and with convection

They give us hope, they give us promise, they
pray for me and you, and for her
I lit the candle over and over for her and her
family, I prayed to our mother, Queen

The flesh is weak, the spirit is strong, I pray
tonight for the world, and the sick
The addicts, the homeless, the poor, the rejected,
the prisoner, the silenced, suffering

The world doesn't center around me, I am a
grain of sand, my soul is still important
He doesn't forget anyone of us; we are all parts
that make up the whole, the painting

The imperfect, our imperfections are made
whole, the painter, poet, and songwriter
They come together telling a story of truth, the
illusionist and destroyer, eliminated

The deceiver tells lies; truth is bypassed by
unfaithfulness and false imagery
Pornography steals the night, steals the screen,
paints the picture, sings the songs

The day will not be taken by the evil one;
the voices of the angels have spoken
The night is divine; it was made for him
and him alone; he rules the world

Love is the weapon, peace is his language, hymns
for heaven sing loud from heaven
We fall upon our knees, hearing the saints
and angels sing praise in unison

Emptiness will be replaced by his promises,
life giving waters, bread of life
Our yesterdays will fade along with our
errors and mistakes, our old ways

Ways that were once our truths, but now are
just the past, in the rearview mirror
Rest is our new friend, we will run and not
grow weary; he will hold us up

Blessings will be found in the wounds that
seem to never heal, tears wiped away
Our trials will only make us stronger, what
doesn't kill us makes us stronger

I no longer pray for myself, my pain is
redemptive, I pray for you and us all
His mercy will shine in the darkest of places,
this isn't our home, my friend

Storms arise from the setting sun, winds;
gusts bringing warm summer wind
We dance together in the midnight sun,
no star to be seen up on high

Waiting for the inevitable to come full
circle, lighting flash across the sky
Tension grows between each glance; our
eyes clash in view, frustration

I lash out in these times, instead of embracing
and cherishing each moment
The given gift that it is, pictures frame by
frame through our eyes frozen

Revealed is what lays underneath, my
emotions speak unspoken language
Without words, without signs, my soul
tells the story of a thousand years

Trapped in my prison cell daily, cannot escape
this skin until the final trumpet
Death though temporary is our escape, so
uncertain but intriguing we ponder

Excitement fills me inner self in anticipation
of the storms tides rising
Quietness though for a short moment relaxes
me, puts me in a trance, tranquil

The feel of the cool damp midnight air fills
all my senses, summers coming end
Finality it seems so certain but in the big
picture the circle is ever more

Continuing round and round until time has
made the final coming, God's peace
Others mock at him, laughing in his face
saying, where are you, reveal yourself!

He is a patient God; waiting for all the pieces
to come together upon his call
As the poison fills their veins and the night
takes their souls, I wait upon you

Like the cool water enters my being while I
thirst during the journey through desert
Your life waters fill me with life; your body
and blood sustains me throughout

A new day begins, I think about you sleeping
peacefully, anticipating the rising sun
We once embraced each other, now the pages
of destiny's trail pull back slightly

What was once so certain, I find doubt, I
find weariness in the journey of life
Things seemed destined to be, I foresaw
ecstasy, romance, and warm embrace

Ignorance is my only friend, not knowing the
overall big picture keeps me sane
Knowing the implications would destroy
my will, my reason to proceed on

Simplicity is what I seek, questions lead to
more questions and less direction
The paths spin out of control into the maze
of this life, I reach out for his hand

The night sky black without a star, moonless
night, I see using my intuition, senses
I see myself in heaven alone on a mountain
top, winds whispering all around me

I also fear that this mountain of eternity, being
alone is my destined hell; by myself
In a place without residence, a place without
laughter, solitude receiving no response

I sit here alone; this is my hell, without a
mountain, no embrace, no sleep, no rest
I pray upon valleys, hills, green pasture, cool
river streams, crisp, air, but with you

With you I can rest, my tears would wash
away all your pain, your distress
Your mansion is beyond earthly description here,
I have prayed for you before myself

For your wealth; you're well-being above all, safety
in the night, protection from all evil
My mansion is my tent on the outskirts of the
desert next to your lush green lands

Luke is his name, he's kind, he's honest, he's
humble; he looks upon us with loving eyes
There's a storm brewing, I felt it before on the
shores of the two lakes, winds churning

The pictures lost forever but the images burned
upon my mind for eternity, hold close
I walked upon the ancient sacred shores, souls
rise, leading me to wear they're trapped

Within prison cells, institutions, where the
insane never rest, alienated by the world
Forgotten, passed by, by the arrogant and blind
of this world, they do not conform

The mind so complex, understanding is a gift,
to be understood is obsolete, absurd
For in trying to make the world think the
way you do, you burn down bridges

The truth is just that, you cannot change truth,
it will either find you or you'll avoid it
Castles made of sand will surely be destroyed
in one way or another, abandoned

Build your house upon the rock; there he will
meet you; saying, good work my son
Wars were meant to be fought between savages,
countries were meant to be protected

Savages are the scum of fallen angels plan from
is to set aside man's common ground
Men were put here to protect our woman, a
phalanx keeping out the wolves, rapist

For the enemy seeks out the woman, her seed
they look to destroy, distraction
I plead to heaven this very morn, intercede,
but I've done this once before, I failed

Cutthroat words, clashing forces, hostility
without unity, silenced my point of view
Wars within our own walls built by ourselves,
both seen and unseen, the chosen few

I'm angry and hollow, can't seem to make my
point, my mind distorted I ramble
The ways of this world are bizarre; I point
the finger and stare, laying blame

We build up imaginary fortresses, walls coarse
blackening out all light inside
Within our walls, shells in which we're concealed,
I doubt and fear daily, I start to cry

The air tonight is thick all around me, these
silent screams piercing my desires
I give into the trials of the darkened spirit, the
truth I seek and knowledge to acquire

I'm ashamed of my place in this world, I feel
constricted, useless and unwanted
I seek purpose and meaning, someone to
appreciate me, I'm suffocating within

I blatantly lie to others, telling them all is well,
stumble upon my words, I'm flawed
My error is filling in the emptiness with nothing,
useless information, distraction

The weight upon my shoulders is heavy tonight;
    I ignore my maker, all of the signs
The story unfolds before my eyes; pleasure
    my enemy, cannot seem to unwind

Forgiveness is what I desire, both for my own
    sin and for the sin of my brother
I cry out to heaven, take this pain away, twisted
    point of view, unveiled, uncovered

Allow me to take your place; I'm undeserving,
    feeling I'm falling out of your grace
Please give me light, I'm dying, this hurts so
    much, we need you here now, Lord

The journey's end has brought me error, she
    soon will be gone; I'm losing this battle
My throat aches, I want to go home now, the
    night brings the shadow; they hide

Once I had promise, where is that child? He
    was fearless, always bouncing back
Malleable, taking punches without complaint,
    turning the other cheek, they mock

I long for peace and the acceptance of my
    salvation; I'm my own worst critic
I can't seem to ever be satisfied, I'm unsure
    of myself; over a year has gone by

The sickness is myself, these pills do not define
    me, there has to be more to me
I used to be surrounded by friends, now I
    spend the nights alone in horror

I cannot save myself, I have no sense of pride;
I cannot make this feeling go away
It's so easy to say just believe, I've been there,
my friend, my future so uncertain

I'm letting them control me, I cannot sleep;
I'm being tested by the fires of hell
My days are spent living a lie, pretending all
is fine within my mind, I'm not well

I fallen into a trap, there seems to be nothing
sacred here anymore, nothing to lean on
I spend my days wishing upon my own demise
and fall, she's around the corner

I'm sleep walking, faking like a dead actor,
ready to fall for the next pretty face
I cannot be trusted to be alone, my eyes
wonder, I'm weak and vulnerable

Sister calls constantly, another lie, another way
to push the needle deep in the vein
She has no conscience, no love for anything
except her next high, I can relate

I know the addict; I've seen through their
eyes, I've thought their thoughts
I've told the lies, hid from the light; poisoned
myself in the shadows, mind rots

The ones we love fall for our threats and
outbursts, they cling onto false hope
The evil one laughs in both our faces, the poison
has taken her mind, she cannot cope

Mind never in the present, always in the past
and future, looking for the next fix
Contemplating suicide, rationalizing their actions,
feeding the habit, slitting their wrist

Nobody loves me, they've abandoned me, I'm
alone left to die and suffer this fate
Pointing the finger, shouting to the heaven's
blaming God shaking your fist with hate

Food and water mean nothing; the drug is what
matters most, how can I obtain it?!
I can't find the vein, where should I put the
needle? They always find a way

Everyone has given up hope, either we believe
the lies or we hold the anger within
Healing needs the healer, the blind cannot lead
the blind; the sick cannot lead the sick

She must crash, and if that means death, then
so be it, prayer is our only option
She must be cut off and aloud to bottom out,
she's made her own choice tonight

What gets her by tonight is banking on tomorrow's
supply which she surely will receive
It comes in the form of cold hard cash without
question, for he doesn't want to believe

This is all too common, our cities and towns
are overwhelmed with this plague
Family's destroyed and torn apart by ignorance
and blind eyes, I now set the stage

The day comes to an end; I'm tired confused,
the world turn's while I lay awake
Eye's wide open, my heart left to take, when
the world sleeps this is my certain fate

Time seems to be standing still; nothing happens
that is new, the same rumor of war
The world will be blackened out soon, the sun
refuse to shine, the moon blood red

They say science explains everything, God is
science and vice versa, we're insignificant
Our minds are so miniscule in comparison to
our Lord, our God, curse our arrogance

We see only a pin drop on a vast portrait, a drop
of water within an ocean, hazed vision
A grain of sand in a desert, a dying star within
a galaxy shinning ever so bright

Yet we explain away everything, our opinions
outweigh God's truth, his teachings
Astrophysicist, scientist of plenty, doctors
pretending to play him, dust in the wind

Digging our own ditches and our graves, mindless
fools, master of our own fate we say
Our human strength will not save us; they will
burn in the furnace of hell for certain

To be the common man, the beggar, the sick,
the lame, one asking for forgiveness
To know you are blind, bowing down before the
king, humble, patient, prudent; wise

Putting others first, living for God alone, these
are things to look up to, my friend
For intelligence has opened the gates of Hades
for the multitudes for generations

Intelligence resulting in pride, philosophy of man
creating fabrication, story, and myth
I met him, he has many a name, he's a gambler,
always ahead, knowing the next hand

He strikes the match, doesn't prostrate himself,
takes, never giving, condescending
He is boastful, taking all the credit, deceiving,
the ultimate user; manipulator

I've seen him in the park; I've seen him in the
Holy Place standing, the food pantry
I've seen him in a crowded room, a party, drinking
and eating merry with acquaintances

He sleeps well knowing the world is on fire,
he's the idolatry; he's the sex symbol
He can transform into the illusions of this
world, he's in the church, in the media

We must wake up and see what is going on,
we must pray now for his intercession
Our Mother in heaven will offer us help;
we must open our ears and hearts

He comes on his throne upon the clouds,
descending upon us in triumph, the rapture
The true church and its people shall rise, pray
not to be left behind, sadly most will

The song bird sings another song, time springs
forth another day, world quietly arises
Soon rumor and speculations will once again
stir, the evil one collaborates, comprises

Violently he looks upon the battle fields using
thousands of years of knowledge
Accumulated, falsifying sacred scripture and
prophesies to suit his every move

The untrained eye, pointing finger inward, taking
responsibility for one's own actions
The day is approaching, the deceiver is uncertain
of the time frame, confusion and rage

Without certainty he blindly makes false
predictions, without any truth or weight
Accuracy is far from being his ally, foreseeing
prophesies of old come true, furious

Using the people of this world as pawns in his
game, they watch upon in fear, anxious
With each chord struck, they listen in fear,
blindly responding to his every request

Discipline is what I seek now; my enemy is knee
jerk reaction, doing without thinking
I mustn't be the puppet they want or need,
molded into a machine, emotionless

I have a bleeding heart, I laugh, love, I play; feel
the presence of the war about to begin
He knows the return is at hand, he sees me,
he watches in the shadow of night

I'm on watch, I'm on call; my Savior has forgiven
me, dying upon the tree, fateful day
We're dead in the middle of the tribulation,
the time is at hand, it is frozen

There is no standing in the way of our Lord;
his mighty hand is outstretched ready
Waters obey him, the tides, the weather, the
crops, man can no longer manipulate

Pain and torture will soon be felt by all; the
scorpions of the desert shall strike
Acid rain, polluted by man's terror, no man
respects another; conflict fills our lives

I hear the storms on the wastelands, the darkened
skies producing no crop or yield
There's no awe left in us, we've become a
predictable society, instant gratification

The sun rises in the east, looking to the east
I pray for there he will return soon
There is no turning back; I lay awake waiting,
for better or worse in my room

I will not be derailed, though knocked down
I will get up upon his request
He is my strength; I shall not rely on upon
myself, but live on the bread of life

Soon I will be on the mountain, grace will
proceed; cleanse me, make me whole
I pray to be burned clean and cleansed from
my sin, for my Savior is in control

Duality between good and evil is mere illusion,
man and woman come together
The races look to the skies now anticipating
our hope, we've weathered the storms

My mistake is comparing myself to the inhabitants
of this world, their accomplishments
My heart belongs to the children, the young
at heart, the broken man and woman

I see them every day, I look into their eyes;
I try so hard to make them smile
To make them laugh, and to feel love, to
let them know it's all worth while

Do they know when I'm not there? Do they
care if I'm not around? I ponder
Would they notice if I disappeared forever?
Over time they'd forget, I'm somber

Sleep walking through this life, unaware of
reality, doing exactly what they say
Constitution slaughtered, burned in the
fire, torched; tossed as propaganda

Destroying the foundation of our great country,
defamation of our founding fathers
The rich faking their way through the media
outlets, increasing wealth, gaining power

Tossing aside the truths of the past, ignoring
lessons taught by history, repeating itself
Forgetting past kingdoms, tyrants and tyranny,
lying, raising money through deception

Lobbyist putting money in the pockets of our
leaders, monopolies doing likewise
Giant companies gaining control, eliminating
human jobs, replaced by robots, machines

Feeding off our habits, watching our buying
trends, our lusts and our addictions
Impulse purchases, inside trading, the elite
getting away with murder, silencing truth

Left wing, socialist education system run by
zombie teachers preying off our children
Sucking like leeches our savings, debt never
being repaid, holding our future hostage

The plan is to divide and conquer, starve out the
masses, reduce the population, control
The evil one has study human nature for
thousands of years, waiting in the shadows

He waits ready to devour the child born from the
womb, out of the desert he will return
He comes with truth upon his lips, a sword
upon his side, ready for battle

The deceiver knows his end is in sight, the rage
and torment is about to be at full force
The male child has returned from a kingly
line, hidden out of sight until now

Consequence and his past is his adversary, our
Savior is his confidant, all understanding
The deceiver will distort the facts; he will turn
what is certain to lies and fabrication

They want to suppress the masses, to question
nothing, accept only their interpretation
Their obscure view point, tarnishing the facts,
filling their purpose and agenda

Controlling the wealth is power; knowledge and
insight leads to psychological take over
Warfare of this kind sways the masses to lean
towards dependence on government

Government dependency leads to a leeching,
dumb downed society, ignorance
Children molded into citizens for physiological
study, lab rats, born to hate

I've seen the afflicted, I've seen the addict; I've
looked in the mirror at the betrayer
I've pulled the trigger, turned away from the
cries; I put our Lord up on the Cross

I've turned away from the prisoner, watched the
sins of man and woman with pleasure
I drank away my pain, I inhaled the cancer;
I'm the hypocrite in all situations

For there is nothing I haven't done; the difference
is that I have repented, reconciled
Asking for forgiveness with sincerity, my
Lord has forgiven me by the Cross

I'm left here in temptation, what to do next, I
am sick and wounded, contemplation
I must take control of my actions, be the man
God wants me to be, respectful

I must lead by example, practice what I preach,
listen to the voice within, silence
The faceless man speaks to me presently, I watch
as the sun begins to fade in the west

The light of the day reminds me of what is true;
the cover of night slowly approaches
I trust no one, nothing; I place my hope in
no man but our heavenly father

The air methodically pushes on, smells of
summer end fill my senses, I digress
Alone, for now I'm at peace and serenity, like
tall grass in the open field moves gently

The glass is half full for this brief moment in
time, like a picture painted serine
The birds silent in prayer, resting sound, rolling
waters, still frame, frozen in time

Taking the afternoon in stride, silent are the
church bells this evening, angels sing
The sun glistens over the glassy waters still,
the troubles world can wait for me

For now my vacation though a day is well spent,
thinking, reading, running, relaxing
The air is cool and comfortable, easy to
breathe, my body feels at rest, at peace

Twilight is upon me, the sounds of the evening
embrace me, opening my soul
The fall of man far off in the distance, peaceful
darkness and quite surround me

There is no tension here; hours have passed
without my acknowledging, time ceasing
Standing still on the edge of the earth, the moon
shines as a sliver, bright in the sky

Clouds spread across horizon to horizon, scattered
accordingly to God's perfect plan
They're obedient in his call, his manifestation;
his picture perfect creation

Forgetting the ways of the world, empty
promises of earthly desire, accumulation
Wealth, power, yet everything burns in
the end, pleasure is overrated

Friends come and go, now I sit here in solitude,
the festivities begin all around me
Families and friends get together, eating,
drinking; my friend tonight is my pen

The church bell tolls, the night passes on, soon
a new day will begin, carry onward
The night is still, I wait patiently for things
out of my control, out of my reach

Out of sight, out of mind; his plans for me
I pray, are immense and exciting
Though fear of the future runs rampant through
my mind, I wait in great expectation

For so long I have felt stuck in the mud, motionless,
living the same day over and over
Time has stopped; the deceiver has no more
vision of the future, only prophesy

Prophesies that will surely come true; his only
companion is fire and his pawns
The whole picture is only seen by our father
whom keeps his secret plan intact

No other has the foresight like our father in
heaven, no one compares, nothing!
Tonight and there after I must choose, freedom
and freewill are his gifts to us

The evil one cannot touch my soul; it belongs
to God and will return without void
I feel the eyes upon me, requesting my fall,
wishing harm to my soul, devouring

I fill in the empty moments and voids keeping
busy, avoiding my downfall, demise
I must keep and open dialog with my Lord,
praying is my weakness, I'm lazy

I turn a blind eye, pretend he's not watching,
continue in my sin, not giving effort
Telling myself I'll get better later, I can start
tomorrow, convenience is my foe

Dreading the next pretty thing that comes
into view, he'll use it against me
Heaven isn't cheap, the battle is now a full
fledge out right war, the night fades

Reality, an illusion to me, I spend my days
avoiding its presence, I'm not the only one
I tend to make myself the center of the
universe, there's billions out there

The centuries that have past I have all but
forgotten its truths, its real existence
Wars fought, men executed, tortured,
women raped, children abused

All for power and greed, wealth of the elite,
the separation of the wolves and sheep
The angels shortly will come down and
rescue the redeemed, I now pray

Reality, my friend, is our history, why we're here,
how we got here, where we're going
We must unite under Jesus, without his
teaching and gospel we will truly fade

Waste away into the abyss, our church must unit
as one, there must be an insurgence
A rebirth, a seed planted in the deepest of
hearts of men and women, a revival

Staying silent would be an atrocity and a
crime, the liars will pay for their sins
Unless we repent, we will truly be damned
for the inner circles of hell

Who founded this country? Why did we cross
oceans to get here? What is truth?
Questions we mustn't forget, our history is
what makes us, and has led us here

Our present isn't something we should
remake, reshape, and mold into lies
Truths of the universe cannot and should not
be tampered with, nor laws of nature

Opinions are useless and hold no weight over
what God has laid down as our foundation
Here, nobody is right, and nobody is wrong,
it's a matter of interpretation, relativity

Wars of the past were fought by fist, bow and
arrows, daggers, swords, cutting deep
Battle axes smashing skull, breaking bone,
fracturing, splintering, blood, earth seeps

Feeding Christians to lions, hanging men from
stakes, crucifying and torturous death
Impaling, setting ablaze, keeping the masses
at bay through scare tactics

Today a push of a button from a drone, guns,
atomic bombs ready to be fired
The wars today are psychological, we're
under false illusion we're safe

They say we're safe as a result of less war; instead
the war is within our family structure
Thousands upon thousands of baby's voices
silenced by the knife in slaughter

Households run by the media, buying and
selling by their rules and standards
Using their currency backed by nothing; digital
coin spewed forth from thin air

The antichrist lurks in the shadows, watching
America tear itself apart through sex
Sexism, the battle of the sexes, black lives matter,
women being men, men being women

Laws being destroyed and altered; America is
the enemy! Terrorist are the enemy!
We all are the terrorist! Both sides wear civilian
clothes, we're both filthy, disgusting

This is not peace; the world is in a state of
illusion, deception, false security
Daily threats of war are false flags, they're a
farce, empty threats to control society

Hurricanes, typhoons, earthquakes, famine,
pestilence are why we should worry
This is what is going to destroy us, along with
us destroy ourselves upon command

In my room I hide, the world closes in all around me, I'm afraid
The door is shut to protect me yet holds
truths, unseen, I start to fade

In my room demons gather, waiting for my
slip up, waiting to laugh, mock
I hold trophy's, articles to keep me safe, I enter my room in the dark

I sit here with pen and paper, reading,
writing, waiting to enter my room
I'm terrified of what might happen tonight, I can all but assume

I avoid the mirror, the cross upon my chest,
thinking of one and only thing
Forgetting my Savior, blocking him out, and all the prayers I sing

Eyes are upon me in the darkness of my room, I fear to rest my head
The stench of death engulfs my room, I
pray now to the cross to be lead

In the light of the day holds truth, the
night is where I can at times hide
In my room he calls me to enter; I hold weakness within and lie

In the distance the light burns bright, all
colors flash across the horizon
Staying in one pin point spot, not moving, stationary it fly's within

Spinning hot, burning out brightly, it fades with the coming of him
Mother and son see clearly off in the distance, the outline, the rim

Through these hazel eyes in look and peer into the dark, he awaits
The traits taken on by our ancestors, letting
us know where we came from

Are they forgotten for eternity, has their
spirit been lost, do we just exists?
We are not just animals, we feel, we're empathetic, yet we still resist

Eyes are upon me in my room, I cannot
sleep, the day coming to a close
I hear the battle cries of inebriated adolescence, the thorn of the rose

Tonight I avoid my room, for there is no
rest; no place to lay my head
I wait here ready for his beckon and call, silence I hear instead

Father where are you? My head falls,
nodding off, I'm restless, unaware
My fate rest in the hands of an invisible
God, into his eyes I pray to stare

Gazing for eternity, bliss in each step I take upon the gold streets
For the day I meet my grandfather again,
all of his children to finally meet

Hidden in a corner, gem to be revealed,
summer now in the rearview
The stakes are high, the days are long; all the time it's been a rue

All these thorns among my side tear my
mind into shreds and pieces
The make me feel old, bring me to low
depths, day's I have on a lease

Drudged and dreary are my blue skies, his
childhood in the woods images burned
His mind for ever seeing his sister run away
into the cover of night, the page turned

Crossing the bridge, under beds, running away
from home, always with another man
Performing acts no boy should ever see, I can't
seem to shake them off, time stands

Still like the nights were I would return home,
never knowing what to expect
Never wanting to go up those stairs; hell
awaiting in my room, I'm oversexed

The picture of the bear in the attic would keep
me up at night, fear of being alone
Sleeping on the couch night after night, in
the desert of life I have roamed

Forgiveness seems so out of reach right now;
I can't even go on to the end
My prison has been forever forged,
I've pretended all my life, now I haven't a friend

I've entered hospitals alive, left them dead
in anxiety beyond belief, changed
Drugged up on medications, I stumble in
the darkness, forever I'm rearranged

I've seen the mentally ill up close, singing and
talking to themselves, treated poorly
Pumped full of drugs, walking around in
stances, they stare back oddly at me

I've judged them, peered into their eyes and
soul, trying to make them believe
I've sat and broke bread with them, painting,
getting treatment, wanting to leave

Get out of the prison cell and walls that surround
us, forgetting why I came at all
Why I walked around for miles, the reason
I was there and why I had to fall

I became humble from the experience,
but came out worse than before
I looked for the vices I once held onto, not
looking at the consequences in store

I was threatened with shock therapy, I saw
the results in a young lady, I feared
Scared straight into making them believe I was
better, ship out of control I steered

Eating nothing but bread and water, wanting
to give blood and marrow
Forgetting my health and hygiene all together,
my mind altered and narrowed

The man on the grate, homeless, cigarette,
disappearing into the foggy night
Riding to Boston, felt I was being followed,
smoking death, saneness I fight

Feeling every moment was a sign from above, the snow, and the rain
Songs on the radio would move me, losing all control, going insane

Praying in the chapel, girl calls the cops,
on me, cousin walks in the door
Angel in the room is gone, I prostrate to
the tabernacle on the cold floor

I am the prodigal son, the Father told me
on that fateful day in autumn
I felt I saw pain, death, suffering, and the
world ending, wars fought in

After my release, she came in my room, I
lay there lifeless; she lay with me
She closes the door, I don't say a word, I
don't fight; she took my dignity

My mind cluttered with thought, feeling
sick, paranoid, can't sit still
Filled with excessive medication, I sit there
crying out to heaven to fill

Fill in the void within, the ache in my
heart and my soul, the emptiness
Better off knowing what is certain to come,
my faith shaken, my laziness

Lackadaisical and content with just being,
not making effort to progress
My prayer life diminishing, tarnished and
in shambles, not passing the test

Though the next step and page would turn, and I would soon fail
My Lord and my Savior would and will always
be by my side, he will not bail

The early morning brings new day, new life, new opportunity await
The mistakes of yesterday gone, they're all
but dust and our past mistakes

Lingering on would be tragic, we would
cast our own selves into the fires
Holding on to what is lethal and poisonous;
listening to Satan and his liars

Change is what I seek, and I ask for the grace this moment and day
I ask for the gifts of the spirit, to cast all my
fears aside, keep my fears at bay

The days no grow shorter, feeling the cool chill in the air overnight
Sleeping with the window open, feeling the
change come forth, land is at sight

Time heals all wounds, these wounds have
left scars I'd never thought mend
Yesteryear is faded though the images linger, my hand I do now lend

There is a way out, a hope, though it may
be most dark before the dawn
He promises certain ever light through and
through, we will not be just pawns

The night song last longer now, as I hear
the first song bird whistle a tune
He breaks slowly out of the evening rest;
our master is surely coming soon

My success and failures he takes upon his
shoulders, I give thanks to thee
For all I have and haven't I give up as
prayer, I bow down to one knee

This morning I will go pay homage, listening
to his word, receiving his body
Given to us at the supper, blood and wine
consecrated for us which was costly

The price was so heavy upon just one man,
knowing his fate for so long
Born to die for our sins, washing away our
transgressions, righting our wrong

She waits in isolation in the cover of night;
bounty's peering around every corner
Waiting for a chapter to end, new life brought
forth from old and the former

Prison will not change her now; she's been
living a hell within her own days
Nights spent in agony, remembrance of
trials of old; should she go or stay?

She has nothing else to lose now, a rat pinned
and trapped within a corner
Hungry, tired, full of rage and pain, the
angst of life starts to storm her

My prayer now lifted up on high, today I
will not be held back in silence
I will fight on to the end; make righteous all of the violence

The threat of war is all around, yet peace
will cross my mind and lips
For he has given me second chances, he has sealed them with a kiss

The snake's head will be crushed by his
heel, wounded and fatal the blow
He will rise up once again, the crowds in awe will now bestow

A poison wrapped in color, into his manner we will give into deceit
Whatever ways he shall plunder, he will sit upon Israel's highest seat

There's a king amongst them, ordinary, like
them in sin and soon will be called
Out from behind the curtain he shall be
revealed, no time left to be stalled

Within My Own Prison

June, July, and August 2016

The sun rises, sets in where time begins
Forever in harmony, washing away our sins

Destiny and fellowship, across our faces full of tears
My wall and my prison meet, counting all my years

The voices of the Angels, sweet with rhythm and rhyme
My ankles in shackles, the day starts with a sign

Shooting for the stars, at times we miss the mark
Failing over and over, the battle starts with a spark

Our worlds collide once again, laziness our truths
The page is wedge and formed, starting from our youth

A sandwich to the poor, the wicked take a stand
I've lived in my prison cell, bottoms where I land

Green paint fairly new, my stomach in knots
When to listen, when to talk, my money is in the slots

A game life is not, for our lives are at hand
In this day I find new hope, to make my final stand

These trials must happen, you will be here soon
Our eyes meet so tender, in your heart make room

Our voices sing as one, your heart so pure I know
The sands come together, stained glass windows

Come with me now I plea, tomorrow we make a stand
Lessons in our lives, on firm rock we will land

Our time is at hand, waters flow like rain
Inside we see the emptiness, and we're all the same

Born into a world that can be meek with horror
This day we'll meet the man we call our Father

Around in circles, love and furry meet
A never ending war of wars, God has won complete

Fear all aside, tears and rivers connect
My love I cannot hide, no more regrets

My soul is accounted for, no more pain or tears
This my life and future held, amongst all the years

Another game, heat seers my inner most being
I wait for the approach; it's now time to show what I'm feeling

Confusion runs rapidly, stealing my strength
My hours collected in time, I must go to great length

Breakfast, lunch, and dinner, sharing, breaking the bread
Our lives intertwined, race, religion, love instead

Victims of neglect, fast forward to the past
Starring into loving eyes, our chances we now cast

Clothes and love, feeding the poor and the naked
Giving each other another glance, our hearts vacant

Light amongst our worlds collide eyes rising sun
Red moons of mars, I'm in the platoon

Fighting for love, the language of the angels
Heaven down from above, the food set by the ladle

In runner in a race without a paddle, drowning waters
The room starts to spin to where is the callers

She's vintage like rampant tides on the sea
We turn curses into blessings, both you and me

Childhood games, flashes of lightening cross the skies
Each breath a second chance with tears I cry

Beauty skin deep, face so pure and clean
Baby hair woman's eyes, scream the morning being

Days, nights, are countless, we will meet again
The warmth of your eyes, in God we will win

Watching movies, listening to music, love hearts open
The day is drawing close, the dawn, my pen is broken

The music silenced for a moment, we sing as one
There is beauty in this world, dancing just for fun

The lights are dimming down, the restless lay their heads
What's once was lost now found, raising up the dead

Moments in the dark, no moon to light the view
The changing of the tides, so tight and led askew

I ponder looking for word, no rhyme or reason
These floors hard and cold, hearts call a new season

The sleep overcome by shadow, whispering winds
Sun beating down upon our shoulders, we must come in

Breaking bread as one, laughter fills my heart
Being with friends we're close, here at the start

Beauty returns in natural color, faces radiantly shine
Sitting in unison the clock roles forward in perfect time

My head feels troubled, walking, hands move forward
The outside getting louder instead of moving toward

The goal is at reach, the chains are running thin
The tears are in my eyes, bone to flesh water skin

My body aches, mind torn amongst the wolves
The night approaches fast, erased are all rules

Stay awake and listen, your life depends on it
This dark and scary world and place where I sit

I hunger and thirst at this hour, the pages wear
Discomfort and arrogance arise, claws will begin to tear

Sun setting in the west, fist pump and wail
This is a chance for freedom, and to set sail

To see you once again, see your small tender hands
To look upon your face, countless amounts of sands

Your eyes so kind and gentle, your soft brown hair
To look upon your face, our separation not fair

To hold your hand tight, your shoulder upon mine
To give my heart to thee, pulled apart in time

I'm scared, tired and weak, as the night approaches
My feet are tired and worn, walking upon the torches

The Beast is unleashed, the table is ready
Contrary to belief, the footstool unsteady

Furry at the dinning, torment began
Love casts its light, forgiving our sin

Twice as nice, three fold and we're torn apart
This day of promise, weakened at the start

Thunder and lightning are on the way
My soul will be replenished, we're amongst the fray

Anticipation for the release, mind don't fail me now
Strain and levers fill my soul, only question is how?

Brand new day given by God above on high
The wind and breeze are new now, starry skies

The air seems strange; the wind feels cool to touch
The night feels unequivocally brighter with heaven above

It's time, the day has arrived, the stars take align
The day has been set, two worlds now collide

I'll see you soon, your beautiful radiant smile
I'll hold you close to me, just one more mile

The water is benign, the faces change and fade
The morning is brand new, through the waste I wade

My past is gone, my future now awaits in glow
The stagnant air lingers, the new sun and moon know

Heaven's peaks arise, faith is my brand new light
My love for my God has gotten through this night

No more tears of pain is where I am driven
No turning back now, all I need is what is given

Today some will leave, though others take their place
The light seeps on in, to the light of your face

I'm so uncertain, these times I'm most confused
My stomach in knots, my mind so confused

I feel God in this place, I awake for a moment
These shackles on my feet, have been broken, now I own it

Tired, cold, misty eyes, no hand to hold
Restless, lonely nights, our bodies given to be sold

Terror sweeps the pastures, fields of yellow gold
Our fate decided a long, long, time ago

Distances measured, obstructed view, children play
The earth is soaring through the night and day

Perfection is the illusion, the table set for all
I've seen it in his eyes, The Great Divide we fold

His passion is our fate, beginning and the end
His passion was for all, so I could call you friend

Woke up this morning to a new song
These chains and locks are on my soul

The birds were singing, and they seemed so alive
But the burden left on my soul, I need to strive

A cup of coffee, just a privilege
How about a cup of water instead?

Yoke is taken off my shoulders
It's no longer just a joke

I pray for you, my friends, to wake up from an early slumber
Jesus is our king, I awake instead of cumber

I see yellow flowers, wishing they would heal
I see yellow flowers on canvas, the Father will heal

The gate is most narrow, reaching to the other side
Calling him by name, this journey long coincides

The garden so full of grace, but not too much at once
I see an old mansion, life filling the emptiness within

Colors that multiply, day in and day out
Feeling serene, the sun fills the empty spaces

I may be wondering, through space and through time
The gate seems so narrow, through time and space

The reservoir calls to me, I run to her beauty
Colors in multitude, green of plenty filled with life
There's a fork in the road, just take in the options

Either way I'm saved, for Heaven rains down
Stone walls, reaching a thousand years, you come around

There's a lock on the door, friendly faces and all
The sadness and illusion, he works around our fall

This day moves through time, galaxy so wide
The gate way to Heaven, all of us will cry

Grace falls upon me with no measure
I pray for a good distraction, it last forever

Seems like so many restless nights
I pray for a storm, that darkness of night

I'm not the smartest guy that ever lived
But I know that the light can't be extinguished, myself I give

I don't have much, my worth is few pennies
But my soul is put on trial, those that have more

Tranquil, complacent, nerves seem to grasp
This heart wide open, this is not supposed to last

Falling into traps, you're about to see for sure
This lock on my soul, will be changed so pure

This night fades slowly, clouds hang low
This table too familiar, these threads I sew

The smells so unclean, my soul burning like ambers
The water is running dry, all that seems left is slander

The chairs never change, the cold slips into the darkness
Decisions I contemplate, the thoughts are so monotonous

Restless feet, low patience level crashing low
Feet amongst falling stars, against the current I row

Aggression takes a stance, mind clustered plenty
The surge of adrenaline rises for the many

Scorching sun seeps into my burning skin
Ocean water twists and turns looking for a win

The rough patch approaches the narrow fine way
Her eyes grow in color, wish I would stay

So tired souls touch close and embrace in peace
Knowing we are fine, and quite at perfect ease

The color waves of hair across your face so pure
Moments like this I always wish to endure

The lion speaks and guides the night sky above
This moment I've been waiting for is really truly love

Your kiss is like the summer rain filling all my heart
It's been you and you alone, right from the very start

Sun rising high, beauty rest from within
Seeing faces unfamiliar, gifts I'm carrying

Love comes from all around, certainly from above
Gifts of food and friend's, His grace is enough

Laughter slender on high, hearts lifted grand
We don't have much to give, other than brother's band

Amounting worlds collide, signature of our will
The sun scorching down, hearts beat as one for filled

Never enter minds of pity, waters in which we thirst
Tardiness is wedged, family erases the curse

Tenderness the key, we all watch and play
Praying this will never end, all darkness wiped away

Our energy attacks the crowd, letting fear fade
For on this holy night, into his arms we'll stay

The air is cool winds blowing upon my face
The day is fair, into the clean woods of space

I blaze the trails of long past far and in between
The flowers, honeycomb, nest bliss so serene

My heart pounds with love running through my veins
The songs of songs whispers in my ear while it rains

New eyes glowing ambers, sometimes I fall
My friends surround me with prayer, I now call

I cannot give in, it's just not in my makeup or will
The world awaits, my chest pounds what is fulfilled

I can't thank enough, for what no one truly deserves
You call and now I answer, remedies I now learned

Grass choked on the roots of weed
Salutations of America, nothing but dead reeds

Money of excess spread throughout the ages
Gold and silver charms seems so damn endless

I have a disease eating away at my being
We are all leapers, blind and not seeing

Part 3

Lost Forgotten Poems

Life Without Love
Jeff and Jeff's Song

Unknown Date

Just to see your pretty face
You know my pulse begins to race
I stare at you but you walk right by
Cant' face the truth so I live a lie

And now my heart it stays so frozen
Cause I'm not the one who was chosen
Gave you all I had left to give
You still make life so hard to live

Sometimes life just isn't fair
But I've got a future and people who care
All these things they mean so much
Which I would give up for your touch

So why do these moments pass us by
For every instance that I've cried
Lying awake in bed so restless
Life without love seems so senseless

Dreams Behold

All this pain, centers within, it can't seem to go away
You are my strength, all the more to stay

It is my fault you got so far, now I cry, I'm all alone
I'll never tell the secrets consumed, keep in touch if only by phone

I'm sold, I'm bought, a hero's only success
I'm yours in time, seems only the best

I came to see a fold or a fraction of what was
Ask myself the questions of what; or was because

Can't see the future, or what it will behold
All I can say, is that it's you I'll hold

I want so much to be, for life I can't predict
With you by my side, I will forever connect

With hope and love, our dreams behold
Without you I'm lost, eternity I'm sold

What I knew is lesser than life, now life's lesson is given
For what you offer is more, all I want is to be forgiven

Lie's all close to the extent that they're true
It's been you since the beginning, it's always been you

Holding by a string, it's what I do best
If it wasn't for you, I'd be nothing but less

Can't wait to be in your arms once again you know
For this harvest you reap is during the season's first snow

Which seems awkward at first sight, first glance
But you seem to move mountains, from your firm stance

A sun set in sight, glowing bright in our world
Your words excite me within, smell of the ocean, begins to swirl

I don't have time for mistakes to excel, leaves on grass
Smells of autumn, come into mind, I'm yours again, so fast

I stare at the ceiling, just before saying goodnight
How I wish you were with me, how I would forever fight

My dreams haunt me, for the days run short
This darkness drags me down; all I ask for is more

For you in my arms, till the end of time
All I ask for is for you, is that all but a crime

Borders, miles, states subtract us apart
But my feelings within, is what gives me a new start

Meaningless shows could never compare
For this is the truth, I will never stare

At another, or close, you are the one
Soul mate, an understatement, you are my sun

Thank you for smells of no compare
You are my strength, in your eyes I stare

Feeling alive in this life is what I strive for
For in your arms, I am nothing but cured

In closing I'm torn from life and truth
My lies are brought back from my scarring youth

My head hurts so, home is what I cry for so
But with you in the picture, I feel less than low

In fact I feel great, only wish you were there
You were always the one, into your eyes I stare

God Sent Tears

This burden is heavy, my heart is light
Shadows run deep, yet I regain sight

They say it has been hidden thru all the years
I can't hold back these God sent tears

Without you there would be less than hope
But with you by my side I can now cope

With this weight on my back and chains on my soul
Though the night long, life begins to unfold

You are the key, with the all-important part
A lead in life's journey, from beginning to start

You brighten one's day, never giving a frown
The least you do for one is never putting them down

A winter's night with crisp, clean air
A snowy morning will never compare

To knowing you once, even just for a day
You're a gift from heaven, how I wish I could stay

To the tops of mountains, I'll forever touch
Because you were there with me, you mean so much

I can never thank you, the way I should
How I wish you could come with me, yes I would

Would hear your voice, angelic with sound
Your beauty shines bright, how I have found

Heaven's kiss with a gentle embrace
Seeing you happy brings a smile to my face

Meeting you has changed my confidence in man
My heart is now complete, warm as the sand

Smells of wood burning, ambers of gold
The fire burns bright, I am now sold

Forever your friend, dying for you
I'll give you my heart, for all in view

To see hearts shine, soaring above
This seems so surreal, like watching a dove

While so radiant, always in pace
Light filling the room, not crowding the space

Space between us, forever more
I'll miss you much, never settling the score

We'll never have between us two
How I'll miss you always, it's always been you!

Words So True

Without you I'm nothing, bare forest no trees
You're simply the one, I fall to my knees

Can't afford much, my hearts what I give
You bring a smile to my face, and reason to live

The pains of time, and when you're not around
Cut through my heart, without a sound

I'm deeply in love, from my heart to my soul
The two I possess are the ones that you stole

My heart bleeds so, my words so true
My dreams sore high, everything is for you

Sometimes I fail, but with you I'm a king
I'm lost in your eyes, all I can do is sing

This love makes me weak; in your arms I'm whole
You are my love, you complete my soul

I try so hard, to give reason to live
All you do is love me, and continue to give

I cry alone, my life sometimes hard
My patience is down, like I've been handed a bad card

This life is tough, but with you there
It's like a lifeline, I know you care

I'll swear I'll be better, I'll never give up
I'll give you heaven, and from that cup

It will never end; I'll bleed from the pen
And we'll look into each other's eyes, and ask remember when

A beautiful song, the perfect rhyme
Couldn't describe you, you're the perfect women, the finest wine

My eyes to see you, my tong to taste
With these senses, I would not waste

A flower in the sun, cool summer breeze
A moment with you; I can plainly see

Tomorrow is nothing without you today
My love it's been you, you're like a flower in mid-May

Like Clay

My heart aches so, for so very long
These tears come easy, it's just so wrong

Hurting inside, too many distractions
Sometimes I'm torn, feel just a fraction

Of what I once was, long before now
I must be honest, and make a vow

To be all I can, not to give in
To give all of myself, and once I begin

I think I will start, where it all began
Where my heart foundation, lays in the sand

The waters pound hard, the surface breaks way
Like a summer storm intense, like the cracking of clay

I can't describe exactly how I feel
All I know is I care, and this is real

You've lifted me up, in times we've spent together
Easy to talk to, conversation that never

Never dull or boring, always with interest
I can't remember when you would be anything less

Less than that God-sent girl, I'll miss you the most
It hurts me so, making sure to never boast

When you're gone, part of me will die
I must admit right now, I constantly ask why

This life is tough, decisions so many
In the end we grow, strong and plenty

Better our hearts, singing out with glee
Being happy to know, the best things in life are free

My soul is poured out in pencil and pen
And the best thing is, you'll forever be my friend

Another Chance

This day unfolds, the night revealed
Radiant are you, as truth is sealed

Never changing, but just as clear
Your heart is pure, and so very dear

Time turns the leaves, change of season
Another chance, I'm given reason

To believe, in hope alive
My inner self is given drive

My faith in God, gives me strength
My soul lifts up, I go to lengths

It shines down, for all to see
An angel so bright, that sits by me

Smells of spring, colors of plenty
Your kind soul, rare not many

That you take the time, to let one know
You're warm and gentle, soft as snow

Crisp and clear, your heart so deep
Your sweet voice, it starts to seep

In my veins, run through my blood
My heart is weak, it starts to flood

With joy that brings smile from ear to ear
You're in my presence, I do not fear

For if I had at least a chance
All I wanted was to make that stance

Elegant, patient, beyond your years
Magnificent heart, refusing to fear

Mind that gives both reason and love
Never putting yourself ahead and never above

Meek and humble, lending your hand
Charisma of plenty, countless as sand

Troubling hearts are put to rest
A gift from God, you're nothing less

No book or story could ever tell
Replenished waters from the well

Life takes turns, like ocean waves
Not holding back, but you gave

Soul to keep, water to wine
You change my view, give back my time

Taken away, from me within
I feel renewed, freed from Sin

In the end that I write
It comes to close, this dear night

I hope I given you at least a friend
You've made me smile once again

Warm, Gentle Heart

Friendship is hard to come by in this saddened world
You're the exception, one important special girl

Your heart is warm, filled with delight
Deep in the darkness the blind regain sight

Sight your soul replenishes your friends
You're a diamond ring with the power to mend

You radiate joy, hope, and love
The Holy Spirit shines upon you like a dove

Stars shinning down in the dark night sky
You spread your wings, take flight and fly

A special place in the Kingdom there is for you
Looking from the mountaintops with the perfect view

Not a selfish bone you ever possessed
For your heart is pure, nothing less

Christ took special care in shaping your soul
An angel on earth He forever told

Told a story where happiness prevails
Eternity is at hand, you shall forever sail

Into the heavens, in breathtaking bless
Your soul dances, God making a list

A list of good deeds that never ends
You are selfless, treating all as your friend

You're a song in the morning, with perfect tone
With Christ at your side you are never alone

You make me smile with a warm, gentle heart
Having everyone's attention right from the start

Where a desert is dry you bring the rain
Giving the rest of us hope, keeping us sane

Washing away bad days is what you do best
Putting a smile on my face, you do nothing less

Whatever your plans, I can plainly see
You make everyone better, including me

In closing words I just want to say
Everyone's better off knowing you, you brighten our day

Green Pastures

Love is immeasurable, nothing less
Arms wide open, completely selfless

Knows no opponent, only embraces
Coexist with Truth, true to all races

Filled with warmth, tender and light
Unforgettable visions, rapture, and delight

Praying this feeling never loses hold
Of someone so beautiful as you are so bold

Never lose sight of that one important love
Who gives nothing less and disguised as a dove

He will come again and again holding you close
Reminding you to take a chance, but never to boast

Except in Him, he will hear the words
Of incomprehensible thanks of the Lord of Lords

You give us hope in a world so dark
Hope that last for eternity, ignited by your spark

Green pastures with gold on a sweet spring day
Compared not to your soul, how I wish you could stay

But you leave us soon, once come spring
Forever we will be friends though, this the Angels will sing

When I see the snow and its quiet fall
I imagine your smile and its gift to all

Your touch is healing, it is plain to see
You are filled with Karma, I'm on my knees

Praying that God will bless you ever so deep
With never ending gifts that you for eternity reap

The stars shine bright but still they are dim
Compared to your beauty that radiates within

The greatest time of year is when Christ is born again
But close behind there are you, only God can send

Send to your friends a special gift, arms open wide
To the rest of us a smile that warms us inside

It doesn't really matter anyway what anyone else says
It just matters that you're here right now and my friend always

Spaces in Between

A storm in brew, lighting flash
My mind at ease, the rain falls fast

Colliding thoughts, can't hold back
These words I say, all out of whack

All I want to feel, my fears lash out
You by my side, it's all about

Your strength is felt, all inside
I'm sick with fear, I start to hide

Insides hurt, mind aches with pain
I'm all but steady, all but sane

Can't change what's real, saved within
My heart beats fast, holding all in

I want to say, be by my side
All I do, instead, is hide, I hide

Your face shines color, I watch in awe
The feel or touch, my cries the flaw

Whispers in this night, ache my soul
I talk to myself, and start to fold

Thinking of what's right and wrong
Stand by myself I sing this song

T.V. stares without you there
Spaces in between, I continue to stare

Don't know when the end will come and go
With you there's no telling, I'll never know

Your words making me feel alive again
Sarcasm refreshing, from friend to friend

Your eyes so deep, brown with fire
Your soul uplifting, with deep desire

Skin, hair, so perfect to say
The moment is right, so right today

The night so right, if words could tell
Troubles are near, I could never sell

The right words to speak, near you I'm weak
I'm torn within, so very meek

I'm shy, screaming one last word
With this I say, I'm free as a bird

Finding Truth

Though your heart aches, filled with pain
My hand reaches out, all the same

Just ask yourself, now and then
The answers within, here is when

It hurts sometimes, the road is long
But when God is by your side, you cannot go wrong

Tension runs deep, fire burning slow
There is a reason, it's just below

In front of your eyes, it has always been
Just breathe deep, and stay close to your friends

Love ones never leave, giving you hope
Giving you comfort, so you will forever cope

Problems sometimes big, but never breaking spirit
For your love is immense, all near can feel it

When you are lost, just look up and pray
Then you will find truth, today is the day

Stepping from darkness, into new found light
It is what you must do, never stopping the fight

The struggle is so real, in these empty times
But please don't give up, don't commit the crime

Of standing still, letting hate consume
Please do not fall, to this evil doom

If you need a friend, ask and you will see
For as sure as the sky is blue, you have a friend in me

Sometimes we fall, hurting soul we cry
Getting up is tough, but we must give all and try

Never holding back, our talents and our hearts
Sometimes getting hurt and going back to start

To begin again, steps small but steady
You'll know right from wrong, and you will be ready

To make that choice when thrown your way
Live first for God alone; and it starts today

A pack for life, for all to grab hold
Please don't give in, and be so very bold

Rising above, the challenges of life
Is what you will do, being sharp as a knife

In the decisions that are set forth
Use what God gives you, use your warmth

Your gentle and kind, never lose those gifts
Use prayer as your guide, and always wish

For when you wish, you hope not holding back
For in the end you'll prevail, this is given fact

To Lauren

I heard the news, it's sad to say
The best is always taken away

To see you leave breaks my heart
You will always be a vital part

Of my life, forever more
You, I will forever adore

It just seems like yesterday
That I met you, I'd have to say

It's been worth it all, I plainly see
You just mean so much to me

You never gave up on this poor soul
For this I thank you, I'll never fold

I'm off guard, my defense is knocked down
You're a part of me, can you hear the sound?

Of God's voice, He's here to say
I'm here with you for always

I'll follow you until the end
You are my forever friend

We have cried but never gave up
Drinking from life's cup

Our eyes meet with everlasting love
Encouraged from the One above

It's been awhile since we met
It's not over Lauren, so don't you forget

You've given me so much hope
I'll have to say you got my vote

When my heart hurts, feeling sorrow
All I think of is that tomorrow

I'll see your face that God sent
It's plain to me that it was meant

Meant to be for you and me
I'd have to say with us there's victory

For we've continued without fail
The sea sometimes rough but continue to sail

You are the key in all of this
At the top of my best list

I'll never cease to proclaim
My love for you, we're one in the same

Christ is born tonight again
Second best is you, my friend

I've been blest to know your heart
From up until now and right from the start

They say it's just a drop of sand
That it's not much when in your hand

But I'd have to say it's much more
For it is like all others, is accounted for

"Christmas 2005"

The day unfolds
This gift of gold
Opportunity revealed
The move is bold

Yet it is set
And then the pull
Is made for all
Once starved now full

Blind now I see
For once I could not
You are in the mist
Of what is now a full crop

This is what
Must be for your future
The future is now
And you must not soupier

Into the hands
Of falling upon
Disease of stalling
Breaking the bonds

Of once must formed
You now fall away
For the old is just that
The news here to stay

Your hands the vice
Writing forms of beauty
Stretches are much
Feelings of plenty

Feeling sets in
Your love gives warmth
Sounds of the night
Gives strength to the storm

A storm of lights
This day proclaims
From thought gives birth
From nothing comes fame

Do not give up
This search of hope
Desire now found
And now I cope

With land in sight
Now in reach
I see the light
From land the beach

A young girl
With much to give
With all the world
Much more to live

For all to strive for
And much more to die
Beauty skin deep
Though this one is my

My friend so close
For this is the day
The answers up front
And is at bay

I am so close
To answering the question
That has been asked
Up till now has been mentioned

Now that it has
And now I can see
For it has been told
And I know I must be

The friend with smile
And firm hand of strength
It is you I must calm
And must go to lengths

To see you must
The flow so steady
Of focusing
And now so many

Questions of so plenty
And now the end
Are all but rough
Grateful you're my friend

We all but can
'Cause after all
The shift now
Is all but failed

The new is now
But come to stay
It now has come
It's now come stay

Winter Solstice

Dreary skies, snow falls deep
Nights last long, forever sleep

Head hurts, why? Tomorrow comes
Hurt so much, you feel the numb

They say relax, your day is near
Sit in silence, your only fear

Fear to move, feel the sun
The warmth of Heaven, to be all but done

Mistakes of plenty; fill the air
Life hurts so, you sit and stare

But hear me now, I stand and plea
There is much greater, without a fee

Pray, my friend, and you will find
There is a Heaven, and with it kind

People of Love, with outstretched arms
Looks of Love, with beautiful psalms

There is a God, with purpose at hand
Warm embraces, with soft cool sand

A mother extravagant, with God's warm smile
An angel's touch, with fields for miles

People run thru soft warm clouds
Smells of pine, with promise so loud

God's face looks down, on you for awhile
Giving you hope, and a brand new style

That only He can give, loving you deep
If you knock you shall find, just seek

The answers within, He gave us this day
For tomorrows a prayer, listen and stay

Lights of beauty, skies of color
Smells of forest, being kind to each other

The moment is yours, the time is right
Get on your knees, and pray this night

For He is listening, and doesn't back down
You are a gift, and not just a sound

The love is within, and remember today
God's won our hearts, and now you'll say

At the end of the night, one last wish
For the movement to last, and that one true kiss

Our prayers have been answered, for He really did send
A gift; a diamond, yes you! A wonderful friend

The Sacrament

I missed Mass today, I feel so down and blue
It's not that I'm torn; it's just my blurry view

Things seem to be, less than whole in sight
I reach far back within me; this is one I must fight

My Lord says listen, wait and you shall see
Stay in your present-now, be all you can be

Patience is what you must, pray for now and ever
And you will be great because, time you will endeavor

What you see and hear is only for the few
Hold my hand from this point on, it is what you must do

Without hope without prayer, there is no tomorrow
But with these both there is today, and now you must borrow

Advice you must bring forth to the entire human race
For it's within you'll see my heart, and friend you'll see my face

Giving in is nothing less, than tossing in your hand
So just reach out and grab mine; there are more grains of sand

On the shore of life's beach, the wind toss and turns
For with me on your ever side, you will never burn

Give yourself and much more, you will soon agree
There is nothing you cannot have, nothing you can't be

The days exist, the moon shines, why? I've proclaimed!
That they came to be, I am not ashamed

Of your birth, I knew you much before you ever heard
I made you long ago, long before the birds

In the sky I come in awe, the stars above you shine
For in this moment I set forth, I give the gift of wine

Peace and silence rest within, the seas are calm and smooth
Island breeze hush of soul, my life is touched and moved

The smell of pine in winter's month, snow falls down with grace
You can't put me anywhere else, the greatness of this place

So when my heart aches with pain, and I am lost and weak
I'll think of you the redeemer, I will search and seek

This is the day for you have made, my journey starts here and now
To give you honor, praise, and love; this is my vow

Stars Light the Night

Time weighs heavy, sometimes so dark
The hour is near, forever is the mark

Eternity enters my mind, the dawn is close
With you in the shadows, you're all, the most

Doors open and close, music sets the way
Eyes open wide, as sun lights the day

A perfect setting, stars light the night
In the distance there is hope, for love I fight

Walls so thick, choking life's hold
Avoiding the punch, I'm bought now sold

Into your hands, the nest is so warm
I don't want to leave; your mind has now formed

The mold is perfect, never letting all see
My heart melts, for all I want to be

Is yours in this life, all I want is happiness
For with this comes tomorrow, and mind comes wellness

Getting by isn't enough, for strides move forward
Behind the scenes I fall, I try to move toward

Obstacles move, swaying in the wind
I'm a tree rocking back and forth, looking to send

The seeds of life, just to carry on
This cycle repeating, I am so fond

Of your tenderness, knee bends and folds
Could you be the one, to you I hold

Warm and gentle, your candle shines laminating
I go back and forth, sometimes so frustrating

Wishing, hoping, the days run far in between
For the future looks hopeful, and I hopefully I've seen

Brighter days ahead, it just has to fall
The pieces are set down, I've heard the call

Cool air hits my face, it goes to the end
Not only have you won my heart, you are my friend

This room so small, I'm tired sometimes weak
All I want is room, and to find and to seek

I wait, feel, and pray for the moment
The time is near, and I now own it

With arms wide open, my mind there to
Your eyes tell the story, and now clear my view

For while this comes to a close, and the day changes pace
I look to the heavens, this is a must-win race

Hand in Hand

We walk together hand in hand
Ocean breathes light, the night soft sand

My heart has hit hard times, this one could save
Cool air in the night, repetition in the waves

Waiting in the past, leads up to this day
My defenses laid down in everything you say

You don't hold back, this seems so real
My worlds brought back to life, I can finally deal

Reality jumps up, biting me, waking
Kissing you is a dream, now I'm not forsaking

My soul lifts up, while I stand here and pray
I hope you don't let me go, I hope you'll stay

I've gone thru hell, and wished for an answer
In your eyes there's peace, they'll be nothing greater

Shocking beauty, but still I hold on
For change with light deep, this life is gone

Out of my reach, until you came
My body aches, this still picture frame

Hoping you feel the same, all that crosses mind
All I think about is the aura, and how kind

You are you know, don't let them say
You are striking I shout, and if I may

I can't stop thinking, about your face and moves
You never hide; I fall into your groove

Nature's beauty could not compare
The whole world couldn't offer, it's not fair

I could not be, without your presence
You light up the room, I have a life sentence

That I would not give up, even for it all
Thru those eyes, I can't do nothing but fall

Into that smile, rich and plentiful
Your moves so elegant, and I'm so mindful

The pressure weighs heavy, my burden is light
For you I'd move mountains, yes I would fight

I cry in the desert, for water I thirst
With you in my arms, my soul all but burst

The day is new, that night has past, and when all is said and done
I hope for in the end, is the chance you'll be the one

This Prisoner of War

Call it luck of the draw, the cards laid down
This is how it unfolds, your voice the sound

I hear from afar, there isn't another
The smell of the fire, with sister and brother

Harmony in sync, wind in your hair
Can't help myself, can't look away, I stare

Into the abyss; this is almost fine
Rich and whole, your soul a fine wine

The finest to offer, reserved for one
My weakness in you, knocked down I'm stun

Walking down this street alone
I sit by and wait, down by the phone

Nervous and helpless, can't be patient nor free
A prisoner of war, I'm so very weak

I scream aloud, no one's hear to listen
To be by your side is my only mission

Your voice so gentle, your hands so warm
This feeling inside is a frightening storm

Raging waters, to the sea I am thrown
Into the waves, I'm new, I'm reborn

Velvet snow, soft, crisp, and clean
Into my heart and unto the scene

Is this truth, and above all great
You and me both, looking at fate

Pleasure and pain, mixed all together
On a warm summer day one never says never

It may, could now happen, that it might
Hand in hand we walk, isn't that a sight

We've both made mistakes, I've said it before
But I tell not a lie, it is you I adore

You I respect and wouldn't let down
You're a glimpse of heaven I'm glad I found

Life would be boring, needless to say
You're my strength, and if I may

Ask you a question, uplifting and more
To forever and back, I'll forever soar

A Gift from Heaven

The wait was long, but in the end
You are my love, and my best friend

Struggle hurts my heart, but with your love
You make me glow, like a sparkling white dove

The day is long, my knees are weak
For your touch, I start to seek

Your smell, your touch, your gentle ways
I hold you close, never want to leave, I stay

A little longer; just one more minute
I kiss your face, I cannot stand it

It makes me high, I start to smile
With you by my side, I'll stay awhile

I can't afford the world, but with my pen
I'll write a poem, and won't fold or bend

You give me hope, you give me reason
You're my fantasy, you're the fifth season

The sea, the forest, the winter's air
With you by my side, we're the perfect pair

Your blue jeans and summer dress
I love every part of you, you're simply the best

Girlfriend I could hope for, the summer rain
Naked in your arms, there is no pain

The brightest star, in the sky
Could not compare, I ask why

Why do I deserve a gift from heaven
Like water to tong, like lucky to seven

Like wine in my veins, you're my drug
Your soft warm smile, even a hug

It's not just this day, I think of you
You're elite amongst all, one of the few

February 14, 2008

The night is silent, the wind breathes light
Your kiss awakes me, all through the night

Winter air crisp, ever so clear
This one is so close, ever so near

My heart breaks within, screaming aloud
This is my promise, I make a vow

To go till the end, far and beyond
This is what I'll give; I'll write you a song

Forever a gift, from me to you
With passion and love, you're among the few

Who listens intense, without backing down?
An angel's voice, I hear the sound

From nights on the roof, to walks on the beach
Hand and hand, I'll forever reach

Dinner and a movie, walking down your street
Moonlit walks, I will never meet

Anyone like you, forever more
Will touch me so deep, we have much in store

Your smile breaks me down, touching me deep
Making T-Shirts together, sweeping me off my feet

Your hair so soft, graceful motion
The room so bright, love like potion

Six months of bliss and a lifetime ahead
The journey goes on, from each other we're fed

Flowers, candy, and cards can never describe
How I feel for you, I'll never hide

When I need to talk, you're my best friend
When I need a hug, always there to send

The affection I need, that you clearly have
You give to me, you never make me sad

And at the end of the day, when I'm laying still
The last thing on my mind, the last thing that fills

My head and my mind, will forever rest
You are my one and only, you're simply the best

To Erika and Josh

2006

Two hearts meet, making one great love
A love that shines bright, as radiant as a dove

Peace is your tool, in creating this life
A life that is pure, like when you asked her to be your wife

It shall never end, this bond between two
This endless joy with a perfect view

Amongst the angels is where you belong
Never ending hymns of love and praise, this forever your song

With parents like you this child is blessed
Like in the arms of the creator, the child will be nothing less

When you pray for miracles, God smiles with content
He touches your soul and now considers it sent

Love doesn't fade, it only grows in time
The harvest is now ripe, now is the vine

The vine of life which forever gives light
To all which ask, the blind now regain sight

Things happen for a reason, the time is now
This union is perfect, now renew your vows

Your vows of love never leaving one's side
Forever in one's arms you're on life's ride

It doesn't stop here, now there is another
You've both been given life always in wonder

A new page is turned, the slate wiped clean
Faith is your guide, let God intervene

Joy in your heart, warmth in your soul
There is so much to give thanks for, having no control

Control of emotions for what you truly feel
The day awaits, you both drop and kneel

Await this gift; you'd wait for eternity for
The answer is close, right at the door

Never give up on what this life gives you
And if you follow this, consider it a virtue

I wish you well and nothing less
Congratulations to you both, I pray for the best

Part 4

The Rant

The Rant

November 6–10, 2017

The light is now gone, extinguished is the flame
Dreadful are the darkened moments, letters lost in the shuffle

The nights are long, no warmth by the fire, it is all but gone
My friends, acquaintances scatter, sickened are my thoughts

Fractured memory torn, frail, too much for anyone to handle
The addictions were overwhelming; I feel the pain of their souls

Getting back to where we once were, importantly whom we are
It is the difference between life and death, face down in a ditch

The chanting in the night keeps peace within the mind
Whispering words, giving strength replenished body and soul

Though we have the power to decide the story has been foretold
Seen only by the power of God, we're reassured our fate

A destiny not predetermined, but given to us as choice using reason
How the young cut throat like Cain, murderous indeed, cursing

Poisoned minds, corrupt darkened hearts, blackened with cancer
I've peered into their eyes; nothing lays there in their hearts, selfishness

Entitlement is in their nature, without hesitation they pull the trigger
Answering only to their own call, one grounded without foundation

The cornerstone is absent from their lives, the ego dominates
Money is power, though debt is the reality consuming them

Their temples disguised as beauty are made of filth and rot
The stench of death rises through their fallen empire, lands of waste

Substances filling their egos are their only companion, shipwrecks
Obnoxious their cruelty, baby minds not fully developed, filled with pride

Experience they lack, skills developed are mere mimicking what they see
Their perception is a false reality, placing faith only on the physical world

The unseen is obsolete, its existence mere fabrication; blurred is their vision
I've looked in their eyes; they feel immortal, invincible, without flaw

Compassion is absent from their beings, the devil has many names
This lost generation is a result forgotten discipline replaced by ego

Our flame has now been put out, though a spark will start our hearts again
Hope is something we shouldn't take for granted, fear shakes the ground

My hands unsteady as my life moves through time and space
Unable to stop the moment though in the grand scheme is miniscule

Pushed to the edge, the fight within my being is irritating my nerves
The last that I have is frayed, worn, I'm beaten, jagged are the rocks below

Blood stains the floor where I lay; the graves are maxed out to the brim
They cannot hold anymore shells of men; man has worn out their welcome

The shifts in the change of season move sunrise to sunset, celestial
Stars in the sky align to their exact movements charted by man over
time

Though placed there by our God for our calendar, planting seasons
As the darkest day approaches I sit and ponder, he comes like a thief

A thief in the night, ready to strike at an unknown hour, be ready
On guard am I at all times, cleaning up my act, repenting, making
whole

Reforming, becoming what I once was, disciplined, listening anxiously
He's in the raindrops, the dew, and the snow falling softly to the
ground

The air crisp with chimney smoke, sitting by the fire, glow of ambers
I sit watching the children play, friends gather round like any other
day

Putting off everything, instant gratification, patience going array
Wondering into uncharted territory, my mind lost in the moment
at hand

Her eyes like chestnuts, heart filled with cheer, laugh like no other
She moves like the wind, going where she is called, a child's wonder

My head pounds with furry; I call out the heavens above in anger
Why can't that be mine? Why must I go what I go through? I'm lost

My compass is broken and destroyed, devastated my mood, my
thoughts
The night brings a certain comfort, the day brings anxiety, and I'm
tired

They lash out at me with condescending words, undermining me
My decisions are under a microscope, analyzed, picked, torn apart

Jealousy fills the hearts of men, nothing makes sense, tear-filled pillow
The bookcases in disorder, disheveled, papers scattered all around

The night seems to last forever, I hear the television play a familiar
tune
The time falls back to change nature's course, manipulated by man

The shelves are filled with the knowledge of the fallen, unspoken
Silenced are the truths of the righteous, intellect confuses the student

Distracted, misinformed is the learner, our behaviors charted,
exploited
Exposed and naked we are found out, our words are our enemies

Caught up in the constant battle of the magnetic pull, polar opposites
Coexisting in a world that seems to by control by darkness so cold

Touching, scratching the surface, persuading the mindless to follow
We march like ants in a line into the traffic, like moths to the fire

The runners take the line bunched up, all in their own heads, alone
What is their motivation? To whom do they answer to, listen to?

Egos take over our lives, comparing what we are to what we could be
Lost in the hollow empty space we consume, we flock together

Separating only when it benefits our own selves, we take pride
Building ourselves up, making our own pathetic lives look attractive

We say we have meetings, we have no time; our schedules are booked
In reality we always have empty space, space that is sugarcoated

Our stink is covered by perfumes, odors most pleasant to our senses
We have not anytime to give to the Creator, the one who has suffered

The morning brings forth light sooner than before, a new day begins
My mind is erased momentarily until the realities seep into play

One pill pulls me in one direction; where? I do not know, guessing
The other pills do something I'm not all that familiar with, I sigh

He enters the room, I do not know this man anymore; he's changed
He hates, he fears, he hesitates, he procrastinates; sleepwalking

Two steps is the dance, though I don't know the number I'm engaged
Programmed to be what they want me to be, I walk in the dead of
night

I sleep on a bed of thorns; rest my head on a pillow of cold stone
Listening to the footsteps of a man that once was dignified, respected

Chatter has calmed down to white noise filling the room, my ears
Tender the touch I give to thee, for my love is real, I'm compassionate

The door has not been shut, time has stopped for all, and mine has
come
I now follow, responding to his call in the night, recollections of past

Turmoil fills in the empty spaces, I pray for justice to come to all
The saints, the righteous, the few have been waiting for the day to
come

The light seems to dim out at times, overshadowed by moonless night
The stars fail to shine behind clouds of grey, whispering across the
sky

The clutter all as one, blinding out what is pure, the cold season arrives
His return is eminent; I start to obey his commands, his request

The laws from our fathers before take hold in my life, our lives
She lays awake tonight eyes wide open, fully knowing the consequences

What is at hand is our future, our hope, the truth mustn't avail us
A hand has been dealt; the dealer knows the game all too well

Counting cards is out of the question, we have been here before
The man in the half suit sits, ponders, waiting for his next move

Timing is everything; the magic trick is a false illusion, the matches
The sleight of hand is his go to, the cigarette is lit, disappearing act

The church is closed yet he searches without ceasing, the prodigal son
He sees the destruction of the future, chosen the moment set in history

Wearisome he makes his way through the church, Mary staring back
Mother and child living for eternity, her smile never lies or folds

Standing in a holy place wormwood storms off in a hostile manner
The future has been set and foretold, the devil and all his furry

I have not a single penny left, all I have is the love between us both
For I've placed all my eggs in one basket, I've exhausted my resources

There seems to be no hope left, I ramble, I rant as the night goes on
The fires of Mordor burn with rage of the enemy tonight in the evening

The ring takes its toll on us; we cannot and will not continue because of it
I am weakened to the core of my own self, left in shambles, in the gutter

She hides in the shadow of the night, her beauty like no other
Physically the curves from her hips and her skin perfect in tone

Her hair silky smooth, her voice angelic, smells of incense fill the room
Eyes captivating, no man can resist her demands, she's supple and warm

Her clothes are of fine material, conforming to her body like no other
She has the answers, appeals to the masses, idea's perfect on the surface

She declares war on who she wants, cuts throat with the sword
Kings, poor, old, young, and everything in between turn to stone

Though she is perfect on the surface, the demon underneath is grotesque
Bleeding puss from her pores, filth and foul stench, demonic plague

She will lead the nations to destroy one another by fire and brimstone
Sleeping with whomever she pleases to obtain her goal of destruction

No man can say no but the chosen few, the chosen one shall prevail
The devil's time is short at hand; his moves are in the future near

Time has stopped for mankind, now you and I must decide our own fate
Each day I'm given my decisions get tougher, the questions difficult

In the chair he thinks about yesteryear, how he wishes to get it all back
A new beginning, an escape, avoiding certain tortures waiting for him

Eternal fires await him; he's terrified as should be of the unknown
Demons come for him in his sleep, telling him there is no way out

Telling him he can't avoid the fate he has forged himself, selling his soul
Once upon a time his life had ended, yet he gave it the devil as collateral

He tries to escape the pain but it relives him daily, he cannot let it go
The books have no answer, his friends seem so content yet they're in prison

The prison cell in which we all live, trapped inside our own skin and bone
As the final days approach, he is reminded of what once was, her beauty

She promises him eternal life, come to the light, yet there is only darkness
Knowledge of the world is his power, the pull of the devil his weakness

He denies himself of what might end his life short, thinking he'll live forever
Reminded every moment of every day, the end is near, get prepared

Prepared for the inevitable, for our redemption, for our salvation, promises
This isn't something we should live in fear about, but celebrate what's to come

The stars now fail to shine; few are left in the night sky for us to see
The constellations we do see are the ones that have stood out from the heavens

Her beauty will be unimaginable, conforming to every man's ultimate fantasy
Every woman will adore her, young and old; she will believe in our duality

She watches my every move, collecting what I have learned over time
My interests, my passions, my addictions, my lusting, what I've let go

She'll remind me of where I've been, how I could go back if not cooperative
Illusions fill the night, the day, the break of dawn and dusk, gnashing teeth

She is the prophetess, the foreseer, the magician, the master of puppets
Knowing the past like no other; connecting to the now and the future before us

Do not tell this woman your secrets; she will use them against you
She will dance in the moonlight for you, fulfill your every pleasure, you'll perish

Once men fought the wars of men, now women fight the wars without recompense
They once long ago created the very art of war and the skill of combat

Pain tolerance is beyond that of mere man, torture is their skill, mentally, physically
The day has now come, she awaits, ready to engage, vengeance her only friend

Desperate are our decisions, time has all but run short, the call is now upon us
Blasphemy she speaks of our God, creating idols of gold, incense of perfumes

Covering the blemishes underneath, makeup made by the deceiver
The beauty of her long hair, sucking the souls of men, leading them astray

The prophetess will set spells upon her prey like a spider spins its web
The blood of men will spill over into the rivers and oceans; she will bleed man dry

To the gallows dead men walking hang, wishing, reminiscing of better days
Days filled with sun upon their face, the sword now pieces the soldier's armor

Like a knife a blaze cutting through butter, men are slaughtered by the masses
As many are brought down with the sword as diseased, multitudes from famine

Bombs fill our nation, homes, offices, schools; we are preyed upon like animals
Books of knowledge destroyed, history repeated once again, only faces change

The latest phones financed by the ignorance of our youth, we're blinded
The young ladies fair skin and tone pave the way for all paid expenses

The young man, the business man, the deceived take the bait; dogs are trapped
They salivate at the chops, looking, searching for whatever they can grab

They gladly take the leftovers; putrid smells fill the halls of those once respected
Voices softly spoken too tender to deny, take and take, never give in or share

The dark angels possess powers beyond earthly measure, their image, the beast
Men have been led into the desert to die for thousands of years, begging

Pleading for mercy, never to receive even a drop of water, everything taken away
Gold stolen from their grasps, hearts trampled upon; the twinkle in her eye

I'm left naked, I'm left damaged, I'm left alone forever until I reach the gates
There I hope to receive my salvation; there I will meet my partner, my Lord

The gate is narrow, the Sheppard watches over the sheep, none left behind
Upon the mountain I climb, in the fields I run, I cannot escape his love

Whenever my head hangs low looking to the ground in disgust I raise my head
I raise my head to see his hand reaching out for me, beckoning me to come forth

Come home he says, finish what you have started in me, I am your servant
Take pride away from my days; make me humble so I can be in your grace

Mountains rise from the depths of the oceans to peek out of the ocean
They rise slightly giving what seems as fertile ground to stand, yet it's cursed

Do not trust what is not stable; do not build your house upon sand, unsteady rock
The glass house shall crumble and fall, smashing into unrecognizable pieces

Play with fire and you will get burnt, the burns may be fatal if one is foolish
The fool believes his ways are righteous until he finds himself over his head

Over his head in grief and buried within the same ditch he made to find cover
Cover from the gunfire, cover from the storm, cover from all his enemies

Alcohol permeates and courses through the soldier's veins, altering his mind
Logic and reason are all but vanished; the same comes routinely in our lives

Lives lived every day, relationships falter as a result from the storms created
Licensed to kill, predators on the move watching each and every step

The fire is burning brighter, hotter; the flames draw all oxygen in
It's getting harder to breathe, the eye is upon us always watching

The children unaware are used, manipulated by the sorcerer, devils
Comfort is found only in the dead of eve, silence is in the comfort, I wait

Questions arise; what should I reveal, and or how much? Wheels churn
The last mile is always the hardest, Calvary's hill not so far away

Eyes wide open this preparation song burns like incense to heaven
They scorn, the laugh, the mock; Judas is lead up the mountain, the hill

The screaming within his own head, piercing sounds, terrifying
He is lead to the tree of death; rope in hand no way out, selfishness

The poison that consumes my mind fuels the receptors with chemicals
The science is not exact, fueled by the puppet master I'm found out

I'm reverting to where I was once before, close to the edge, they follow
My nerves stable, I'm balanced, ready for battle at the present moment

Whom should I trust? I need a companion, is there anyone left?
Now that I know love has avoided my final days I must move on

Though I need someone to confide in, get advice, help me discern
Father be my guide as you were Jesus' once long ago, I'm lost

As I write in these final days I cringe at the thought of the queen
The queen of all liars, filled with the cup of abominations spilled over

There is only one other that knows of my past besides my Lord
We question everything avoiding the true answer, creating wooden gods

The golden calf is most real, and our possessions can control us
It takes over our lives, wanting more and more, nothing is ever enough

Her eyes are grayish blue, her skin golden, and her hair dark and silky
Flawless, perfect image, curves of her body like no other; she's here

Driving men wild, she is a body changer, one to your exact specifications
What do you want, how much? She says she can give it all to you

Money, security, pleasure beyond all belief, beyond all expectation
What keeps me in this place? Why do I stay? Should I stay or go?

Identity is a fraud; individualism is a scam in the eyes of government
One can be erased in the push of a button, I tattoo myself

These markings cannot be forged, distinct like that of DNA
Years upon years of pointing the finger as one lays on their deathbed

Then what? Does one decide the fate of another? Kind words
Words go a long way in the molding and formation of another

Tribes, lineage, family lines not yet broken, forged by his hands
Molded into the man child to come, one to rule all nations

Humble are his ways, lacking only the confidence to rule, uncertainty
What controls the mind; the body or the soul? Decisions must be made

He's here, he answers only to his own demands, he's cleaver
He's charming only upon what he wants, upon his own wellbeing

All else is tampered with, giants from the past, intermingle iron, clay
Adulterous and adulterer's committing acts of fornication

Thoughts impure like the smell of intimacy between the wicked
The vile, the murderer's, swaying the masses through false deception

Sex symbols everywhere you look, perfect bodies, that of eye candy
Forcing men and women alike to sin, fantasies never obtainable

Self-gratification only through buying and selling of oneself
Bodies lay twisted, conformed together as one, yet doubt meets regret

About the Author

Jeffrey has spent the last six months exhausting and engaging most of his nights writing his new book. He is spending most his free time working out at the local gym and running local half marathons and 5K races. He started writing poetry in eighth grade, when he was introduced to a writing project by his reading teacher Louise Brady. He also was greatly influenced by his high school English teacher Jerry Lagadec, who introduced him to the classics; for example, Shakespeare. Up until that point in his life, Jeffrey wasn't much interested in reading or writing at all. He loves spending his time writing in East Freetown on Long Pond where he gets most his influence and inspiration for his writings. Jeffery enjoys long walks through the local trails in his area, hiking in New Hampshire, and generally spending time with nature. He loves being with friends and family and loves nothing more than taking long drives through the country and smelling the natural smells of nature; for example, the smell of campfire and freshly cut grass. Jeffrey grew up loving baseball first, then football and basketball, but whatever sports he engaged himself in, he gave all he had, and he humbly believes he wasn't all that bad! Jeffrey's favorite books include *The Lord of the Rings, 1984, Animal Farm, Narnia*, and mostly anything by C. S. Lewis. The number one thing that Jeffrey is most passionate about in his life is his positive outlook toward the ultimate outcome of the ends versus the means. When it comes down to it, through several of Jeffrey's works, he uses references of the positive to give it honor and glory over negativity that exists in this fallen world.

CPSIA information can be obtained
at www.ICGtesting.com
Printed in the USA
FFOW02n0138200418
46287898-47764FF